long
distance

FICTION
The Anthropologists
White on White
Walking on the Ceiling

NONFICTION
The Wilderness

long distance
ayşegül savaş

SCRIBNER

London · New York · Amsterdam/Antwerp · Sydney/Melbourne · Toronto · New Delhi

First published in the United States by Bloomsbury Publishing Inc, 2025

First published in Great Britain by Scribner,
an imprint of Simon & Schuster UK Ltd, 2025

Copyright © Ayşegül Savaş, 2025

The right of Ayşegül Savaş to be identified as author of this work has been asserted in accordance with the Copyright, Designs and Patents Act, 1988.

1 3 5 7 9 10 8 6 4 2

Simon & Schuster UK Ltd
1st Floor, 222 Gray's Inn Road
London WC1X 8HB

For more than 100 years, Simon & Schuster has championed authors and the stories they create. By respecting the copyright of an author's intellectual property, you enable Simon & Schuster and the author to continue publishing exceptional books for years to come. We thank you for supporting the author's copyright by purchasing an authorized edition of this book.

No amount of this book may be reproduced or stored in any format, nor may it be uploaded to any website, database, language-learning model, or other repository, retrieval, or artificial intelligence system without express permission. All rights reserved. Inquiries may be directed to Simon & Schuster, 222 Gray's Inn Road, London WC1X 8HB or RightsMailbox@simonandschuster.co.uk

Simon & Schuster Australia, Sydney Simon & Schuster India, New Delhi

www.simonandschuster.co.uk
www.simonandschuster.com.au
www.simonandschuster.co.in

A CIP catalogue record for this book is available from the British Library

Trade Paperback ISBN: 978-1-3985-4772-8
eBook ISBN: 978-1-3985-4773-5
eAudio ISBN: 978-1-3985-4774-2

The authorised representative in the EEA is Simon & Schuster Netherlands BV, Herculesplein 96, 3584 AA Utrecht, Netherlands. info@simonandschuster.nl

Simon & Schuster strongly believes in freedom of expression and stands against censorship in all its forms. For more information, visit BooksBelong.com.

This book is a work of fiction. Names, characters, places and incidents are either a product of the author's imagination or are used fictitiously. Any resemblance to actual people living or dead, events or locales is entirely coincidental.

Printed and Bound in the UK using 100% Renewable Electricity
at CPI Group (UK) Ltd

For Fuat, İsmihan, and Adıhan

CONTENTS

Long Distance	1
Layover	24
Notions of the Sacred	40
The Room	56
We Are Here	74
Marseille	94
Ghosts	116
The Guest	131
Practicality	147

Future Selves	152
Freedom to Move	168
Cry It Out	185
Twirl	204

Long Distance

Lea changed the sheets when she got up. She'd bought flowers the previous day, tulips that she'd put on the dresser. There were carnations on the kitchen table, in a squat glass vase. She thought they looked cheerful, and not too fussy.

The fridge was filled with more things than they would be able to eat: olives, jams, prosciutto, cheeses. She'd bought wine and beer, cookies, breads, the round taralli crackers that were common in Roman cafés.

She didn't think they'd be staying home very much—there were so many places she wanted to take Leo—but she had in mind a scene of the two of them eating in bed. Did people really do that? It seemed as though there would be too much mess, nowhere to put your plate. Still, she liked the idea: the sleepy indulgence, the sheets streaked with light—the hour, in her imagination, was late afternoon, which may have been the reason for the beer, though this particular timing would require some planning, with everything else she wanted to do with him.

Her phone buzzed. *Just landed. Will take a taxi over as soon as I'm out.*

I can't wait to get there, she thought, alternatively. Or, *Finally.* But maybe this was Leo's way of elevating the anticipation further, not allowing any release with words.

They hadn't communicated very much in the past weeks, after Leo bought his ticket. Whereas before that they had written almost daily, talked on the phone for an hour, sometimes two. The relationship was still new; they spoke to each other in the hush of mystery.

This was different from their time in California, where Lea had been doing research for a semester. Leo worked as an engineer in a neighboring town; they hadn't met until the last month of Lea's stay. Then, there had been something embarrassing about their late-night returns to her apartment after dinners at the home of mutual friends: a secret, though not a thrill. On Lea's last weekend they'd gone to a restaurant together, to dignify the situation with a formal parting.

But once Lea was in Rome, the emails they exchanged to say goodbye had suddenly become tender. Their messages thickened with a new vocabulary. Lea wrote to him about the city: the banks of the river in the early morning, the market stalls closing in the afternoon, the kiosk where she drank her coffee. She went to small, out-of-the-way museums in part to tell Leo about them, to have him see her as someone curious and passionate.

She was in Rome as a postdoctoral fellow in linguistics. She took the metro to the university—an unremarkable place with Fascist architecture—and ate lunch in the campus café with other researchers. They'd formed a group, and met up on weekends for drinks or hikes. Lea had always felt comfortable among academic types—their measured enthusiasms and logical worldview, their adaptability. But these were not the things she wrote about to Leo. She wanted to portray another version of herself: a young woman in Rome, enchanted by life.

Leo told her that he looked forward to her emails; he enjoyed picturing her in this city he'd never seen, where she seemed entirely at ease. Without their exchange, Lea might have been disappointed in Rome, having always imagined it as something more—more consistent, perhaps, or harmonious. Writing to Leo provided a vantage point, a way to sift and sort, to separate the beauty from the ungainliness.

She went downstairs when she heard the taxi pull up.

Leo stepped out of the car with a clutter of things. Coat, sweater, backpack. Headphones falling off his neck. He was different from how she remembered—smaller and paler. His expression was confused.

Lea shouted some phrases to the driver—thank you, good day, thank you again—maybe too loud, too eager to show off her Italian.

"Hello," Leo said. They kissed, somewhere between cheek and lips.

Upstairs, they put the suitcase in the bedroom, then sat in the kitchen. Leo wasn't very hungry. He picked at the cut-up fruits she'd put in a bowl.

"Would you like to take a nap?"

"No," Leo said. "Then I'd sleep all day. We'd better go out before the fatigue kicks in."

Of course I don't want to nap, he could have said. *We just reunited*.

She put on a jacket over the dress she was wearing, long and sleeveless. She'd bought it last week for this very day. Leo put on his sneakers.

They followed the tram tracks to the river. Lea worried that they walked mostly in silence. Near the Ponte Sublicio, Leo took her hand.

"Farther down's my favorite bridge," Lea said eagerly. "We'll walk it later."

"I trust the guide."

Once again, she was excited for their weekend ahead. Back in California, she'd felt a constant fluctuation of her attraction toward him. The first times they slept together, she'd found him almost repulsive. In their months of emailing, too, her image of him had swung back and forth. Sometimes it seemed that he heard her words exactly as she intended them, other times that he was deaf. At those moments, she would feel resentful: before she arrived in Rome, her friends had joked about all the Italian men she'd meet in the course of the year. She'd felt, once or twice, a pang of injustice, as if her desires had been curbed, her freedom restricted. The person she described to Leo in her emails—a woman enchanted by the world—should by rights be enchanting others. Not that she'd met anyone, though who was to say that she wouldn't, if she allowed herself to look.

 She'd practiced the route to the restaurant once before, and plotted a path there through ivy-strung streets. She commended herself on her pick: the back garden was empty and sunny. The waiter tended to them with cheer, didn't show impatience at Lea's Italian. They got a plate of antipasti. Leo suggested beers. While they were waiting, Lea reached for his hands across the table, rubbed her palms up and down his arms.

 Afterward, they climbed the hill of the Gianicolo, then surveyed the city from the Acqua Paola. Lea told him about the researchers at the university, exaggerating the character profiles for effect. She liked that he listened to her without interruption, kept track of names, didn't contest her point of view when she told him someone was annoying or boring, totally brilliant or a terrible scholar. Back in Trastevere, in the honey-tinted light, they sat down for Aperol spritzes. Their conversation was enlivened by tipsiness, their hands entangled restlessly over the table, touching insistently.

"Let's go home," Lea said. She waved for the waiter. They walked back to the Ponte Sublicio. It was only later that she thought they should've taken a taxi instead.

"Something strange happened on the plane," Leo said as they were crossing the bridge. He had his arm around her waist. Lea leaned into him, exaggerating her tipsiness, making a slow, sensual dance of it.

"There was a woman next to me."

"Ooh," Lea said. "A beautiful woman?"

"She told me such a crazy story."

"I like crazy," she slurred.

"I felt like she hadn't talked to anyone in months. I felt so sorry for her."

"Are you trying to make me jealous?" Lea asked coyly.

Leo stopped walking. He took away his arm. He looked sad, or disappointed, which Lea found patronizing.

"She was really troubled," he said. "She was an old woman."

"OK," Lea said. "You could've just said so. How was I supposed to know that?"

This was, more or less, the end of the conversation. Lea was too proud to ask him to tell her what the woman had said; Leo didn't offer to continue.

Back in the apartment, Leo asked whether he'd somehow upset her. If so, he was sorry.

They were sitting at the kitchen table. Lea was sullen, but preparing to let it go as soon as Leo made an advance. Instead, Leo apologized again, and said that they should perhaps go to sleep.

He was being decent, of course; he must have thought that it would be wrong to make a move, given her mood. In another situation, Lea would have considered it crude, even aggressive. But at this moment his decency upset her even more.

"If that's what you prefer." She got up and went to the bedroom, aware that she was shutting down any opportunity to make up. She changed out of her clothes, put on a T-shirt and shorts.

When Leo came in, she was lying with her back to the door. He fumbled around in his suitcase, tiptoed to the bathroom, slipped into bed. There were a few minutes of what seemed like charged, mutual waiting. Then he was asleep.

Lea thought with frustration about her smooth, soft legs, her lace underwear, now wasted.

THERE HAD BEEN, in fact, one opportunity since her arrival. The researchers from the linguistics department had met up on a Sunday to walk the Appian Way. Someone had invited a cousin—Riccardo—who arrived wearing a leather jacket and loafers.

"Are we attempting Everest?" he asked, surveying the foreigners with their water bottles and sports clothes. He and Lea fell in line and ended up walking most of the path together. Riccardo told her the history of the trail, not suspecting that she might actually know far more about it than he did. Anyway, she didn't mind. He related his vague facts with animation, complimented Lea on her observations and questions, made outrageous jokes about the others. It felt special to be his accomplice. There was a picnic afterward, and the two of them split up to join separate conversations. When they were leaving, Riccardo told Lea he could drop her off, since he lived near her. They went to a bar across from her apartment.

During their second drink, she told him that she was seeing someone. Not to prevent anything from happening, exactly. She wanted to be guiltless in the aftermath; not to have led him astray. Perhaps she even liked the notion of being fought over. Riccardo had put a hand to her cheek. After her revelation, he took it away. Once they'd paid for the drinks, he told her good night.

THERE WAS NOTHING romantic about Rome on a rainy day—not when you hadn't yet seen it enough in bright light. The city took time to get used to. You had to learn to love it without makeup, puffy-faced.

But here it was, a rainy morning. The apartment was cold and damp. Lea brought out the electric heater from where she'd hidden it in her closet. They sat at the table in socks and sweaters, drinking tea.

"We could go to the Palazzo Massimo," Lea said. "Or to the Borghese. In any case, we'll have to take a taxi."

"What would you prefer?"

"I wanted us to walk through the park to get to the Borghese," Lea brooded. "But that's obviously out."

"Let's do the other one, then."

Once they were dressed, he came up to hug her. "I'm really glad to be here," he said.

"Sorry I was in a mood," Lea said.

"I'm sorry, too."

"I feel like I wasted our evening."

"We had a great evening," Leo said. "With a minor glitch."

"I wasn't jealous or anything," Lea said. "I was just being silly."

In the taxi, he told her the rest of the story. Lea didn't interrupt to point out the sights, though she was a bit sad he was missing them.

The woman sitting next to Leo on the plane had been married at a very young age. Soon after the wedding, it became clear that there was something wrong with her husband. Nothing precise, at first, just a sense that he was off balance. He was a meat salesman—that was how she'd met him, on her own doorstep—and she'd found out, on a trip out of town, that he was notorious in all the surrounding counties, where he was known as the Butcher. But it was too late: she was pregnant. After she gave birth, she and her child were held hostage by the Butcher for more than a decade.

"Wait a second," Lea said. "What?"

This was all a very long time ago, Leo continued, and it wasn't entirely like the horror stories one read about in newspapers. The woman still had some freedom, and she'd ultimately managed to leave with her daughter and make a life elsewhere. It wasn't a separation, though; she'd had to escape. Leo added that he was summarizing what had been a very complicated story. Somehow the Butcher hadn't been able to find them again, or disturb their lives.

"You have to stop saying 'butcher,' " Lea said. "This story is so messed up."

"That's what she called him," Leo said. "She didn't want to say his name. But it gets worse. She was actually coming back from the funeral."

"Whose funeral?"

"The Butcher's."

"Will you stop saying that?" Lea said. "And why would she go to his funeral?"

"It was important for her daughter to be there. To have closure."

"Is this woman Italian?"

"No, but she moved to Rome many years ago. She considers it her home. She became a painter, which was her dream before she met the . . . her husband."

"Bullshit," Lea said. "This can't be true."

"It really is. She even won an award."

"She became a painter and settled in Rome? She went to her torturer's funeral after a decade trying to escape?"

"People can start over," Leo said.

"I don't know," Lea said. "It's too much."

"Well, you weren't there."

They'd arrived at the palazzo. Lea decided to drop it.

"That's an awful story," she told him once they got their tickets. "It must have been very upsetting to hear."

They headed to the gallery of frescoes. One room was painted like a garden, lush with birds and leaves. Entering it offered another perspective, cutting them off from the present tense.

When they came out, it had stopped raining and the sun shone brightly. They stood on the steps, looking at the traffic. Suddenly the day felt new, and festive.

"I'm starving," Leo said. They ate salami panini standing at a kiosk, then walked all the way to the fountain of turtles, where they sat in the empty piazza. Leo said he'd be content to do nothing else for the rest of the day; he was feeling very happy. They returned home early, before dinner or drinks.

In imagining the act, she'd forgotten the facts: his rush to get to it—not roughness, really, more like bashfulness; his reluctance to look at her for too long. Back in California, she'd conceded to his haste, hadn't insisted that he slow down or that he meet her gaze. Now she was more demanding. There was a twinge of antagonism in her touch, her hands directing him, yanking at him to stay still. She hardly knew where it came from—whether she was putting on an act or letting resentment seep through.

In any case, it was done. The sex needn't loom above them like an invisible boulder. In the morning they stayed awhile in bed, their skin acquainted, their conversation giddy. Breakfast was jam-filled cornetti at the café downstairs. When they finished their second coffees, Lea suggested visiting the Vatican, or the Forum.

"I'm not letting you leave without some proper, large-scale tourism."

"Get some selfie sticks," Leo said. "Some fanny packs and hats."

Lea liked this new familiarity, different from their emails. In the end they went to the Borghese museum, walked through the park and down the Spanish Steps. Leo had said that they might as well leave the big stuff for next time. This was another happy moment, when he brought up his next visit. They ate heaping cups of gelato facing a church. They both said that they were having a perfect day.

AT THE UNIVERSITY, Leo and Lea's names had become a joke among the researchers. Somehow, the coincidence made the relationship sound more serious, as if two people with such similar names were surely reunited in love, like Plato's soulmates cut in half at creation.

The researchers were meeting up that weekend at a pub in Ostiense. Lea had told them she would try to come with Leo. "If you aren't too busy," the researchers joked predictably.

When Leo finished his gelato, she asked if he'd be up for going to the pub.

"As long as you're not embarrassed by me."

She liked him for saying that.

They walked along the river to an industrial alleyway now occupied by bars. Lea's colleagues had taken a long table at the back. There were baskets of fried foods, emptied glasses. People cheered when they walked in. "The double-L chromosome!" someone shouted. The enthusiasm was not so much about Lea and Leo as it was about the opportunity to bond as a group, in front of an outsider.

Tomas, a researcher in Latin, put his arms around both of them.

"How can we fill your fountains?" he asked.

Leo asked for a beer; Lea, a glass of wine. As Tomas was walking to the bar, Lea saw Riccardo sitting at the far end of the table. She hadn't considered that he might be here; she felt a momentary panic. But nothing had happened between them, she reminded herself. If Riccardo was flirtatious, she could tell Leo that he'd been just like this on their first meeting as well; it would serve as one of her character portraits.

Riccardo was listening to Rebecca, a scholar in digital archiving. He caught Lea's eyes and winked. *Here we are again*, he seemed to say. Or, *Well, well, look at you*. Lea felt a sudden pleasure, as if there were stage lights directed at her.

She took Leo around the table, introducing him one by one.

"Riccardo is an excellent guide to the Appian Way," she said, presenting him.

Riccardo slapped Leo on the back. "Good to meet you, man. Have some of these fries before I eat them all."

It turned out that the company Riccardo worked for used a software similar to something Leo was working on. Lea knew very little about this topic, and was surprised to see the two men hit it off. She and Rebecca had fallen into conversation out of necessity. After a while, Rebecca went to the toilet, then joined the others. Riccardo and Leo were now talking about music. Lea realized with annoyance that she'd eaten the entire basket of fries. She got up and put her hand on Leo's shoulder.

"Oh, hello," Leo said.

"This man's the *man*," Riccardo said. He seemed to have forgotten about the evening with her.

"You haven't met anyone else," Lea said to Leo. "And it's already late."

He might have noticed the irritation in her tone. He probably thought she was acting moody for no reason.

"Let's talk to the others, then!" he said eagerly, as if to a child.

Everyone liked him. They proposed organizing a dinner for his next visit. Leo proposed having them over for fajitas, his specialty. Lea hadn't known about his specialty. She may not even have known that he cooked.

Then he was pulled into another private conversation—Tomas was giving a long-winded explanation of his quest to make a comprehensive map of Umberto Eco's symbols. Lea tugged at Leo's arm and said that they should get going.

"She's the boss," Leo said to Tomas, arms spread in surrender.

"Whatever," Lea said.

FOR HIS LAST day in Rome, they wrote out a list of things they wanted to do. They'd put aside anything requiring lines and tickets, but they decided to wake up early and walk to the Colosseum, to see the exterior before the crowds arrived. Lea suggested the San Pietro in Vincoli, with Michelangelo's statue of Moses with the horns. She showed Leo on the map how they would then be right by Monti, which had a different feel from the neighborhoods they had been to. Leo traced with his finger and suggested a final evening stop at the Piazza di Trevi.

"Isn't that the famous fountain?"

"It's pretty tacky," Lea said. "We wouldn't be able to find a decent place to eat."

"We can come home for dinner," Leo said. "I'll cook for you."

"Sounds delicious," Lea said. She got up and sat on his lap, straddling him. If only he were staying a bit longer, they would fall into perfect rhythm. Something had begun to loosen in the past few nights, though there was still the tug and pull—his hurry and her resentment, one perpetuating the other.

"Or maybe we can skip dinner," Lea said.

"Mm-hmm," Leo said. *If he stayed longer,* she thought, *he might even break free of his reserve.*

IT WAS SO easy for them to spend a day together. They were practical and spontaneous in all the same ways. They went through everything on their list, made discoveries in backstreets. In Monti, Leo bought her a necklace of blue and green stones. Lea had been looking at it when he asked if he could get it for her. She'd been staring mindlessly, but she didn't say that she actually didn't like it that much. She put it on as they were leaving the shop. Leo told her it looked amazing.

They bought wine and mushrooms and rice for dinner, then took a taxi to the Trevi Fountain. They tried taking in the sight, with all the people gathered around.

"Let's have a final gelato," Leo suggested.

"This is probably the worst place in Rome for a gelato."

"It's better than anything I'll have once I'm home."

On a side street, they got in line at a gelateria with rows of neon-colored options.

"This is a tourist trap," Lea said. "The servers aren't even Italian."

"Don't be a snob," Leo said. "I'm looking forward to the bubble gum flavor."

"Can you please miss your flight tomorrow?" Lea said. "We can have proper gelato."

Leo was holding her in an embrace, his face touching her neck.

"No way," he said.

"What's that supposed to mean?"

"No way," Leo repeated. "I can't believe it."

He let go of her. "It's the woman from the plane."

She was standing at the back of the line, in a red dress. She was smiling to herself, as if practicing the look of someone having a lovely time. Her arms were bare, splotched purple with cold.

Lea's instinct was to turn around before the woman spotted Leo. But Leo lifted both arms to wave. The woman cut the line and joined them.

"This is my friend from the plane," Leo said. "And this is Lea."

Her name was Janet.

"Do you live around here?" Leo asked.

"Oh, basically," the woman said, flapping her hand vaguely. "I mean, not so far."

She told them that she came there most afternoons to treat herself.

"It does you good, doesn't it?" she said, and laughed, which Lea found unsettling.

It was their turn to order. The server was in a rush, not keen on letting them try flavors. Lea repeated that the place was a tourist trap. She got pistachio. Leo got stracciatella. Janet asked in English for a cup with strawberry and hazelnut and caramel. She asked for a wafer on top.

"I'll get these," Leo said, and reached for his wallet.

"You're a darling," Janet said. "Isn't he a darling?"

Lea smiled.

"What a treat," Janet said.

They walked together to the end of the street.

"Well, it was very nice to meet you," Lea said. She knew that she was being abrupt, but she didn't want to risk the woman walking along with them. They parted, waving. When they were sufficiently distant, Lea told Leo that she'd been right.

"About what?"

"About the fact that she's a pathological liar."

"Whoa," Leo said.

"She obviously doesn't live in Rome. She couldn't even order gelato."

"She did seem a bit clueless."

"I mean, who would go there for gelato every afternoon?"

"The snob speaks."

"Also, she really didn't look like a painter."

"The snob strikes back."

"I'm not a snob," Lea snapped. "I'm just assessing the situation."

"And what's your expert assessment?" He didn't sound so playful now.

"That you were duped."

"That's going a bit far," Leo said. "Maybe she exaggerated a few things."

"She made up a different identity! That's *alarming* behavior." She was almost shouting.

"You saw her," Leo said. "She's harmless."

"How is it that you're siding with a deranged stranger and being mean to me for pointing out the facts?"

"How is it that you're so upset?" Leo said.

"Because you're being willfully naive."

"I can't take back the fact that I listened to her."

"And why do you think she chose you as her audience?"

"She said I had a kind face."

"Oh, aren't you lucky."

She felt angry, and stupid.

"What's going on?" Leo said. "This is getting out of control. Let's just have a nice evening."

"Why are you so *nice*?" Lea said. "You're so nice to everyone but me."

"You're being mean."

"You feel so sorry for the crazy lady on the plane. You let her talk to you for hours. You propose cooking for people you just met. You spend an entire evening listening to their pointless stories instead of spending time with me."

She considered that she may have taken one step too far.

"Are you talking about the pub?" Leo said. "I was making an effort with your friends."

"Exactly," Lea said. "You make an effort with everyone else."

They were in front of the Pantheon now, frightening and serene.

"This is quite a sight," Leo said.

It was just like him, she thought, *to avoid her reproach.*

"You know that guy Riccardo? He actually came on to me. And you spent all evening chatting with him."

"I didn't know that," Leo said.

"Even if you did, you wouldn't have cared."

"That's not fair."

"You would've cared more that he liked you."

Leo turned to face the building. Lea had an urge to yank at his shoulder, to make him look at her.

"What if I told you that something happened between us?"

"I guess that would be your free choice."

"Stop it!" Lea said. "Just stop it." She was shouting now. "Stop making me feel invisible."

Leo was silent. Maybe he mumbled something.

"You might as well know that we spent the night together." Even as she said it, she thought there would be an opportunity to take it back, explain that she was just trying to provoke him.

After a moment, Leo asked, "Why are you telling me this?"

She was astounded by the question, by the fact that he needed an explanation. They continued walking.

"I'm sorry," she said. "I was upset. Nothing actually happened."

"OK," Leo said. He looked tired. Still, she was surprised that he didn't ask anything more. Certainly, she reasoned without conviction, it was the respectful thing to do.

They went home. They made risotto. They made love. Leo packed his suitcase.

His flight was early in the morning. A short one to London, then another to California. He would have to leave at sunrise. He'd told her that she should sleep; there was no need to get up.

"Don't be silly," Lea said. "Of course I'm getting up."

She lay in bed while he showered and dressed. When she came into the kitchen, he was writing something at the table. He folded the paper, put it under the vase. Already, the carnations were dry.

He insisted that he didn't want breakfast; he'd just get something at the airport. Besides, his taxi was almost there. They went downstairs.

"I've had an amazing time," Leo said, and hugged her.

Back in the apartment, Lea made tea and sat at the table. She composed a mental inventory of the visit, combing through the events several times in a row. Each time, the scales tipped more toward success than disappointment.

In the note folded under the vase, Leo repeated what a great time he'd had. He said that he was looking forward to the next visit, if he was invited. He'd underlined "if," though Lea couldn't quite tell what sort of effect he'd intended. It almost seemed sarcastic.

There was nothing for him to apologize for, and so he hadn't.

Lea had been wondering about something, on and off during the past days. She realized now that she hadn't had a chance to ask: How had Leo responded to the woman's story? What had he actually said to her on the plane? She doubted that he had posed any questions—he wouldn't have wanted to pry, or to say something wrong.

Lea could picture him listening so silently that it wasn't clear if he was listening at all.

She felt, for a moment, on Janet's side, sympathetic that the woman had had to tilt her story further toward invention, to make sure that the quiet, kind-seeming man would continue to keep her company.

Layover

Lara was supposed to have breakfast with Selin, a friend from middle school who had a long layover in Paris. It was eight thirty, and Lara was frustrated not to have the morning to herself before teaching in the afternoon. She loved the early, luxurious hours when she was free to do anything she wanted, which often meant making coffee and going back to bed to read. She hadn't seen Selin in more than fifteen years, though they'd kept in touch a little over Facebook. Selin sometimes wrote out of the blue, having remembered an episode from their school years, or to ask how Lara was doing. Lara had moved to Boston for university, then to New York, before coming to France. Selin would write that she dreamed of visiting Lara in these places. Lara didn't see Selin when she went back to Istanbul. Her trips were short, barely enough time to see her parents and closest friends. She had nonetheless kept track of the general shape of Selin's life: she still lived in Istanbul; she had a boyfriend who resembled her, with a thick mop of hair and a cartoonish smile; she posted photographs of her handicrafts, which received enthusiastic comments from other crafters.

At the last minute Lara decided to put on lipstick. She walked down the stairs of her building and stepped outside. Sunlight lay bright and jagged on the scaffolded building across the street, where work had already started for the day. There was the clang of metal, rhythmic thudding of sacks thrown on the pavement. The wind was sharp on her face and neck. She buttoned up her long coat, a bit thin for the season, and turned to walk to the bistro at the end of the street. She went there several times a week, mostly in the evenings after teaching. Recently, she'd had a date there with a man she met online. For a week or two afterward, they sent each other text messages. When Lara suggested meeting up again, the man stopped responding.

Selin would have to take the fast train from the airport, then switch to the metro. Lara had assured her over email that this was an easy trip, though she could certainly have suggested something more direct. Selin would be tired after her flight from the United States. She was on her way home from a craft workshop—she'd explained the technique in her message, which Lara could no longer recall. She was bewildered that Selin would bother coming all the way from the airport to see her, rather than walking the city alone for a few hours, maybe treating herself to a nice lunch, a souvenir.

The bistro had green mosaic floors and an old-fashioned zinc bar, cluttered with baskets of bread, an orange press, newspapers. Behind the counter, a waiter was drying glasses with a tea towel. *Selin would be enchanted by this place,* Lara thought; she might even think Lara had picked it because it was so charming.

As far as Lara knew, Selin had only been to Paris once, with her mother, when they were in school. She came back from the trip with two pink Breton hats, for herself and for Lara, and stories of the boat ride on the Seine, the view from the tower, the trip to Disneyland. For the rest of the year she talked about moving to Paris for university. But she'd stayed in Istanbul, saying that she didn't want her mother to be alone.

Lara took the table by the window and brought her book out of her bag. It was a history of an artists' commune in Paris in the sixties. The general subject interested her more than the specifics: letters documenting arrivals and departures, correspondence with suppliers, requests for funding from the Ministry of Culture. As she was leafing through the book, she saw Selin from the corner of her eye, crossing the street in a large duffle coat.

"Lala!" Selin shouted, entering the café. "La la la!"

Her hair puffed out in every direction. Her face, too, was puffy, as if she'd just woken up from a nap. She threw her hands in the air and scrunched her nose—her expression, Lara remembered, for anything happy or puzzling.

They hugged. Then they hugged again.

To Lara's relief, Selin didn't have her luggage with her. She'd imagined they might be scolded by the waiter for taking up too much space, even though the bistro was practically empty.

"Should we get the breakfast menu?" Lara asked, showing Selin the blackboard propped against the counter. "It's all the usual stuff, and an egg."

"I can't believe I'm here," Selin said. "Just like we always imagined." Their breakfasts arrived on two pewter trays. Besides the egg, there was coffee and juice, glistening croissants, a pot of jam, and butter. Selin took a photo of Lara and the trays.

"Look at you," she said. "The Parisian."

"How was the trip?" Lara asked. "How was your workshop?"

"Absolutely perfect."

She'd only found out about it by chance, she told Lara. The instructor was a woman in West Virginia who ran workshops out of her home. She and Selin had become friends online. Last summer, the woman invited Selin to join one of her fall workshops, at a discounted rate.

"That's a pretty long trip for handicrafts," Lara said.

"That's what the others said! They couldn't believe it."

Selin rarely took offense, Lara remembered. She used to delight in people making fun of her, as if it were a sign of their affection.

She'd brought everyone gifts from Istanbul, Selin said, cute little evil eye bracelets—blue and green and silver, she chirped.

"Ozan keeps joking that West Virginia will talk about the arrival of the Turk for years to come."

"Ozan's your boyfriend?"

"Lala!" She'd been meaning to write, she said. She and Ozan had gotten engaged a few months before and would get married the following autumn, in Ozan's grandparents' garden on the Aegean. Lara noticed the gold ring on Selin's finger, with a small green stone.

"You'll get a proper invitation, obviously. I worked on a few ideas during the workshop. By the way, my mother sends a big hello."

"How's my role model?"

"Always the same," Selin said. "Set on having things her way." She swirled coffee in her cup. "That sounds mean," she added. They'd had a small argument recently, about the wedding. She knew that her mother was just being protective, but she was bothered nonetheless that her mother continued to ask whether she wouldn't rather wait.

"Wait for what?" Lara asked.

"For someone she likes better." She laughed, scrunching up her nose.

LARA AND SELIN became friends in seventh grade, after Lara's family returned to Istanbul from Geneva. Selin had befriended Lara in the first week of school. Selin wasn't one of the of girls who sat in a pack—their voices rising and falling from whispers to hysterical laughter and back again—but she wasn't picked on, either. She shared her homework with anyone who asked, warning them cheerfully that she might have gotten it all wrong. And there was her mother, who came to school for board meetings. She wasn't like the mothers of the other girls, frilled and perfumed, dressed in the style of their own daughters and too eager to prove their youth. Selin's mother was tall and radiant. She wore high-waisted trousers and vests and smiled at everyone as if she were a movie star. Selin didn't seem to notice her mother's charm—another point in her favor, as if her nonchalance toward her mother was in fact a sign of her own charisma.

Lara and Selin had nicknames for each other—Lala, Solo—and a secret handshake. At lunchtime, they stayed in the classroom, making drawings. They had sleepovers every week, mostly at Selin's. Lara's mother was a fussy host, strict about bedtimes, whereas Selin's mother didn't need prior notice for Lara to come over. She would ask the girls what they felt like eating, and cook something on the spot or order in. She sat across from them at the table, drinking wine. Sometimes she asked the girls if they'd like a sip as well.

"Mom!" Selin would protest. "We're thirteen!"

Selin's parents had separated the previous year, and her father remarried soon thereafter. A perfect housewife, Selin's mother said of the other woman. One time at dinner, when she'd ordered a bucket of fried calamari for the girls, she told them to count their blessings. "If I were a perfect housewife," she said, "I'd make you stewed beans."

Before Lara, Selin had been friends with the twin sisters from 7B, who were quiet, hardworking, and unopinionated. "Those poor girls," Selin's mother called them, for no apparent reason. She was delighted in her daughter's new friendship, said that Selin had finally met her soul sister. She believed in such things—souls and the will of the universe.

"You were meant to find us, Lala," she said. "The three of us are a gang." At dinner, she would ask the girls questions: What sort of boutique hotel would they like to own? What pastries would they serve if they had a café? Which celebrity would they go on holiday with? Afterward, she told the girls her preferences, which Lara memorized, determined to one day make them her own: a hotel with a courtyard and blue mosaics; almond crostata; Daniel Day-Lewis.

Selin's answers exasperated her mother, or made her laugh: a Mary Poppins–themed hotel, frosted cupcakes. "Oh, sweetheart," her mother said, "don't you think you'll grow out of all that?"

The summer before ninth grade, Lara went to a language school in the Loire Valley. Selin's mother had wanted Selin to go as well, but Selin spent the vacation with her father and his wife at a resort. "A sure way," Selin's mother said, "to kill every last brain cell."

At the summer school, Lara joined the other students after class to go to the village bar and drink lagers. In a matter of weeks, she'd grown tall and skinny. Her tanned shoulders were sculpted beneath the straps of her tank tops. One of the English girls showed her how to line her eyes. On her last evening, she and a boy from Spain kissed on the riverbank.

In the fall, the class split up for science and social studies tracks. Lara and Selin were only together for French and geography. Lara had become friendly with Defne, a member of the pack, and often joined her for lunch. She still slept over at Selin's from time to time. At home, the girls reverted to the way they were before, making up songs, drawing fictional maps.

SELIN HAD FINISHED her breakfast and ordered a cappuccino. "This café is lovely," she said.

"It's not too far from where I live," Lara told her, though she didn't say she lived down the street. "I thought you'd like it."

She pointed out the mosaic detail on the ceiling, the brass window knobs shaped like leaves.

"Crazy how you and my mother have the same taste," Selin said. "She would adore this place."

"Not so crazy," Lara said, "given that I basically copied her style." She felt sudden tenderness for her friend, their familiarity. She asked for another coffee as well.

"She's still glamorous," Selin said. If there was anything about the wedding that excited her mother, it was the dressing up, and all the decorations she'd thought of for the garden.

"I'd want her to plan my wedding, too," Lara said.

But Selin felt uncomfortable about interfering too much. There'd been other weddings at the family plot—Ozan's younger sister and cousins. They'd all been modest events, occasions to host neighbors and family. Selin hadn't yet confronted her mother about it, and imagined it would cause more tension.

"But that's my own problem," she said. "I just have to get it over with. Anyway, what about you? What happened to that handsome man in your profile pictures?"

"He was a photographer. I mean, he *is*. It ended on its own, nothing dramatic. Honestly, I'm enjoying being single."

"Single in Paris," Selin said. *"That's* glamorous."

When they finished their coffees, Lara suggested going for a walk.

"What about your class?" Selin asked. In her email, Lara had written that she would have to teach later, without specifying the time, in case she wanted an excuse to leave.

"That's not for a few more hours," she told Selin. She was now considering canceling the class. They could walk to the river, get drinks. She reached across the table and held Selin's arm. "It's so good to see you," she said.

OUTSIDE, TWO MAJESTIC clouds were suspended in the sky, framing the sun. Lara and Selin crossed the boulevard, then turned onto a side street, where Lara showed Selin the large blue doorway behind which was a Benedictine convent. Lara herself had only glimpsed the inside, the garden and cloisters. She'd heard that you could visit the grounds on certain days of the year, when it was open to the public, though she hadn't been bothered to look it up. The city was full of such places. Their inaccessibility had charmed her when she first moved here, as if it were an invitation to explore, to make the city her own.

She'd come to Paris with an artist research grant and met the photographer in the final months of her visa. They admired each other's self-sufficiency, their mutual lack of neediness. The photographer liked to tell Lara that he'd never had a partner before her who didn't rely on him for fulfillment. After her residency ended, Lara moved into the photographer's apartment. When her visa expired, they got married. Lara's parents came from Istanbul, and the four of them went out for lunch after the ceremony at the municipal hall. The relationship was over by the following summer. The end crept up on them, announced itself of its own accord; they accepted it without a fight. The photographer took a project in Estonia, to document abandoned sanatoriums. He and Lara agreed to remain married until Lara got her citizenship. Lara moved to a studio apartment, found work teaching and guiding private museum tours. Her clients on the tours were mostly wealthy older couples who liked to show off their own knowledge. Lara complimented them on this, showed enthusiastic approval in the banal, repeated facts of art history—that Michelangelo freed the human form from blocks of marble, that Rodin had taken credit for the work of his lover, that Cézanne had truly paved the way to Cubism.

They had arrived at the park of the observatory and stood watching the fountain of galloping bronze horses.

"I love seeing these places," Selin said. "From now on, I'll be able to picture you in your habitat." She suggested taking a selfie to send her mother. They huddled their heads close, both of them squinting from the sun. Selin showed the picture to Lara before sending.

"So cute," Lara said.

Within seconds, Selin's mother texted a line of colorful hearts. *You two haven't changed my darlings. Kisses and hugs.*

During high school, whenever she saw Selin's mother, Lara felt uneasy, as if she'd been caught being deceitful. But she also had the sense that Selin's mother approved of her new social circle, her matured style. It seemed that this was what Selin's mother would have wanted for her daughter as well, and that Lara had made better use of her potential. One time, she told Lara that she reminded her of her own student years. Lara had cut her hair short and was on a drastic diet. "I had just your style," she said. "And your spirit."

They'd reached the end of the park.

"How did you and Ozan meet?" Lara asked. "At university, right?"

"No," Selin said. "Ozan didn't go to university."

It was, of all places, at a summer resort, where she'd gone with her father and his family.

"Your mother hated those resorts."

Selin chuckled.

She'd noticed Ozan with a sketchbook and pen at the beach bar every morning. She went up to him one day and asked to take a closer look. The drawings were so intricate, of bridges and boats.

"I can't imagine you being so bold," Lara said.

"A moment of folly."

Ozan worked on a cargo ship and wanted to get a captain's license. For years, they saw each other once a month, sometimes not even that. The previous year, Ozan had moved in with Selin. After the wedding, they would move south.

"Closer to the sea?" Lara asked.

"Actually, he doesn't work on board anymore. But we'll be closer to his family."

Lara thought that she sounded evasive, and assumed that Ozan must be unemployed.

"What does your mother think about the move?"

"She thinks it's a waste of our youth."

Selin looked at her watch. "I guess I should get going." There was some place she wanted to visit before she went back to the airport, she told Lara. "And you probably need to go to your class."

"I could cancel that," Lara said. "We could have a drink by the river."

"That's so tempting," Selin said. "I would've loved that. We have to plan a proper reunion."

Lara asked where she needed to go.

A bookstore, Selin explained, that specialized in art books. She wanted to get a few for Ozan.

"I could come along," Lara said.

"Don't bother, it's across the city."

"You should have told me," Lara said. "We could have met around there."

"I loved seeing your neighborhood," Selin said.

"Can't you order the books online?" Lara was sad that they would be parting so soon, when it seemed that they'd just fallen back into their old rhythm.

"I guess I could, but I'd like to see them in person."

"*I* think," Lara said, "that you'd like to go for a festive drink."

Selin smiled. The bookshop, she explained, sold large-format books, with magnified details on every page. She spread her arms to show how big. Two years ago, she went on, Ozan was diagnosed with early retinal deterioration. In front of his right eye was a black spot that was slowly spreading. He could still see clearly with his other eye, but it was a strain to look at things for a long time.

"But he won't go blind?"

"He will," Selin said. She was a step ahead of Lara now.

"I'm so sorry," Lara said, too loudly. "That must be very difficult. But it's so special that you stayed together. It's really wonderful of you."

They stood at a crossing, waiting for the green light. Selin looked at Lara but didn't say anything. Then she pointed to the metro entrance ahead.

"I can probably get on at this stop," she said. "I'll figure it out." As they crossed the street, she took a photo of the metro with her phone. These metro entrances, she told Lara, with their green lamps, were among Ozan's favorite details of the city.

"Actually," she said, "Ozan and I came to Paris for a weekend last year." She hadn't told Lara, because she wanted Ozan to do whatever he wanted in the short time. They spent a whole day in the Orsay and another walking along the river. That was also when they discovered the bookshop. At the time, Ozan protested that the books were too expensive, and in the end they didn't get any.

They stood by the metro steps, the green metal stalks of the lampposts rising above them.

"I loved our morning together," Selin said.

"Solo," Lara said. "I'm so glad this worked out. Let's get together when I'm in Istanbul."

They hugged. Then they hugged again.

Lara waited as Selin went down the stairs, and waved at her before she disappeared inside. Then she turned and started walking back. It was a glorious afternoon. When she was back in the park, she sat down on a bench.

Selin would be on the metro now, counting the stops until she had to get off. Lara would send her a text in a little bit, to thank her for coming all the way. She would repeat that they should get together, the next time she was in Istanbul. Perhaps she would visit Selin and Ozan in the south.

She wondered what Selin would tell her mother about their meeting. She might describe the café, say that Lara looked like a Parisian, with her red lipstick and long coat. Selin's mother would ask whether Lara had a boyfriend, and how she'd reacted to the news of the marriage. Selin wouldn't tell her mother what Lara said—that it was wonderful of her to have stayed with Ozan—because she didn't think like that, weighing and measuring kindness. That much Lara had understood, in her friend's silent reaction.

She took out her book from her bag, flipped through the pages, then put it back. It was too cold to sit outside, and her coat was too thin.

Perhaps she would cancel her class after all. She might go home and read. She could always go back to the café for lunch.

Notions of the Sacred

I once heard a woman say that immediately upon finding out, she'd felt the dawning of a strange inner power. It seemed as though she could undertake any task, could live through any hardship. This was a strength not of muscles, the woman said, but of light. In this new form of herself, she felt more alive than she ever had before.

She was recounting all this once it was already over, after she'd had an abortion, but her memory of that brief experience was still tinted by her encounter with what she now believed to be immortality.

The woman's story stayed with me, and I thought about her words when I myself found out, searching my body and mind for signs of my own power. I can't say that I felt it, not in the way that the woman had described, but I certainly sensed a shift, as if I'd entered a different dimension and would from then on inhabit two worlds at once: one steady and flat, and the other mysterious, with depths I could not yet fathom but knew were there.

The day I confirmed the news, I had taken a test and gone for a checkup, too. A stroke of luck found me an obstetrician who was available to see me that same afternoon. She conducted a scan and told me that everything looked good. I left her office feeling elated. On a whim, I entered a shop and bought a felt hat, wide-rimmed and peacock green. It was impractical, more costume than accessory, but I wanted to mark the day somehow—my entry into the new dimension.

As I walked down the street wearing the hat, I saw people glancing at me, and I beamed at them, full of my own mystery, like a benevolence. I thought of the face of the Virgin Mother in scenes of the Annunciation, and had a new understanding of her inward gaze, at once present and far away.

That evening, I attended the birthday party of a former colleague. He lived in a northern suburb with his wife and two children. I cycled to the party, as I did to most places. It was a pleasure to be testing my strength under these new circumstances. I had no doubts about my decision, even if my situation—single, in a foreign country—might appear difficult from the outside. Perhaps, I considered, this was the power that the woman had been referring to—this certainty that I would manage.

There were many people I didn't know at the party. It seemed that my colleague and his wife had formed a large community, though they, too, were foreigners. I could identify the friends who constituted their family here: the ones who were affectionate with the children, those who were putting away dishes in the kitchen, the woman who brought out the cake, making a joke of my colleague's age before presenting it to him.

Usually at such events, I'd be filled with a desire to talk to everyone I found interesting and simultaneously overwhelmed by the effort it would require to do so. Whereas on this evening I felt at ease. I was involved in conversations but not overly invested. I kept remembering the faces of the Annunciation, their calm dreaminess.

On the table of drinks, I found bottles of nonalcoholic beer. It would never have occurred to me to offer such a thing at a party, though I gratefully took one when I arrived. On my second or third bottle, I was approached by a man I'd identified as belonging to the inner circle of friends. Earlier I'd seen him take my colleague's young son and swing him high up in the air, to the child's wild delight.

Don't get him so worked up before bedtime, my colleague's wife had chided, though she also seemed amused.

After we introduced ourselves, the man asked me whether I belonged to the German or the Greek school. I told him I was neither Greek nor German.

That's not my question, he said. I wondered if you belonged to the German or Greek *school of thought.*

Pointing to my beer, he said that the German school believed, out of superstition, that keeping a pregnancy secret in the early stages would insure the well-being of the baby, whereas the Greek school favored telling as many people as possible, to call on the protection of the community.

I feigned shock at his question, though I was, for some reason, neither shocked nor offended. I accepted that the man was flirting with me, in some unusual manner. I felt the same benevolence I'd experienced in the afternoon, when I'd beamed at strangers in my green hat, and I didn't deny my condition.

It had never occurred to me, I said, that women kept the news a secret out of superstition. I'd always assumed it was an outcome of patriarchy: if anything went wrong, it would be considered the woman's fault. Besides, women needed time to negotiate with their workplaces, to secure their positions, because their employers generally treated their fertility as a liability.

I see, the man said. You're probably right. I realized he was surprised that I'd taken his comment seriously. He must simply have meant to tease me about my drink, not knowing he was onto something.

In any case, he continued, I would place you closer to the waters of the Aegean than to the forests of Bavaria.

And I think, he added, that this is a very fine position.

Once again, I didn't object to his words.

For the time being, I had no intention of informing the man I had slept with. It had been a brief affair, and I could readily imagine his distress at receiving the news. I didn't have the patience for it, nor was I interested in any sort of commitment he might half-heartedly propose. For now, I wanted only to enjoy my new state. I walked to the park in the early mornings; I spent evenings reading in bed. I went out for lunches on the weekend, sitting on café patios, chewing my food slowly and deliberately. It was early spring, and the trees were luminous with papery leaves. In the mirror I saw myself as part of this resplendent moment, even though I felt very tired. Perhaps this was what the woman had meant about the power that came over her: this sense of fragile beauty, but beauty nonetheless.

Some months before this, I had become reacquainted with Zoe. She and I had been close friends at university and had lived together for several months after graduation—a time that we later mythologized into a golden era. It was true that back then I thought of many people as close friends, because our relationships had not yet been put to any test. And although it seemed that Zoe and I shared much more than our youthful enthusiasm, we had grown apart over the years. One of us had achieved early success and flaunted it carelessly; the other had made an unfair comment that traveled through the circles of our mutual acquaintances. There'd been no reckoning or drama, but we both knew that something had turned sour. Still, we kept in cordial touch. Neither of us wanted to sever our bond completely; we would certainly cross paths through work, and we could not afford to be hostile. We followed each other's life on social media, and it was always with curiosity that I came upon Zoe's news. In photographs, she looked confident and warm. I liked this person, and I found myself missing her, wishing for her to be in my life again.

Zoe had recently moved to a small town nearby with her husband and came frequently to the city. She was the one to send an email, suggesting that we meet for coffee. The first few times we got together, we were both guarded. We spoke of our achievements with false modesty, complained more than was necessary about our careers. Then Zoe sent me a message announcing that she was pregnant. Years ago, she'd undergone a serious surgery that put her fertility at risk. This had always been a sincere point of contact in our friendship—Zoe's worry that she would not be able to have children—and with the announcement of her news, our past grievances seemed to vanish.

The next time Zoe came to the city, we finally reconstituted our old connection. Zoe was now in the fourth month of her pregnancy, expecting a girl. She would have told me weeks before, she said, but there was such a taboo about sharing the news early.

Which is just awful, she said, because it leaves women feeling totally alone.

I was glad for my friend and for our renewed closeness, which finally felt untainted.

So it was with Zoe that I first shared my news, excepting the man at the party. Perhaps I wanted to talk to a woman in a similar state, as if she could offer protection through her kindred position.

I wrote to Zoe asking whether her daughter would have any rules regarding cousins coming to sleep over.

What!! Zoe wrote back. *What are you saying?!*

Immediately, she called me and switched on her video.

We didn't have a habit of speaking on the phone, and the gesture touched me. We were both teary-eyed onscreen. I told her about the affair, and about my scan. I shared with her my feeling of belonging to two different dimensions.

Oh, my goodness, Zoe said. There is no better way to put it.

We complained about the unfairness of not being able to drink alcohol, not even a glass now and then, because we'd been warned that the risks of moderate consumption had not been properly studied. If men got pregnant, we said, the effect of every drop would have been documented. But complaining was also a way of expressing our contentment. It was, perhaps, a ritual of sorts, to ward off the evil eye.

I'm so glad you told me, Zoe said. I wish I'd shared with friends earlier. But I'm so glad we're in this together.

She kissed the tips of her fingers and blew on them. I blew kisses back.

In the coming days, we exchanged frequent messages. Zoe told me to honor the space I was in, to be gentle with myself and listen to my body, surprising me with her fluency in this type of language.

The next time she came to the city, our meeting was even more enthusiastic. We sat on a restaurant patio, both of us in long, sleeveless dresses.

You and I are so connected, Zoe said.

She was in her sixth month, and her hands moved often to her belly, pulling down the fabric of her dress, as if to assert her condition. We ordered grilled fish, and—as a joke or celebration—asked the waiter if the restaurant had nonalcoholic beers.

Over lunch, Zoe told me at greater length about how she had conceived, without any intervention, thanks to a careful diet and daily meditation, though she had been told by several experts that it would be difficult.

Your body knows how to heal itself, she said, and it hears your intentions.

As for me, I'd hardly given the matter any thought. It was an accident, even though it had recently begun to dawn on me that my time was running out. Still, I hadn't proposed anything to the men in my life, had not considered IVF or freezing my eggs, even if I could have afforded to. I'd done nothing more than abandon myself to pleasure.

Which just goes to show you, Zoe said, that these doctors don't know anything about the miracle of our bodies.

I wasn't quite sure what she meant. After all, I'd never consulted doctors, though they would probably have told me what I already knew, that I was past the limits of youthful fertility. Still, I didn't object to what Zoe was saying. If anything, I encouraged the conversation: the wonder of our synchronicity, the way it had happened so naturally for us both. There was the sense that we were special in our good health, in the blessing we had received. I didn't acknowledge our smugness then, or if the thought occurred to me, I brushed it away.

I HAD NOW shared the news with a handful of people. These announcements felt like gifts I was offering, letting the recipients know that they had an important place in my life. And with each I felt a thickening around me, of joy, perhaps, or love.

My mother had already decided that she would stay with me for the first few months after the birth. On the phone, I recounted every new discomfort I felt, and my mother cooed and soothed me.

From time to time, I told her Zoe's news as well. What sort of birth she wanted, her plans for returning to work, the curious new ways of her body. I jokingly scolded my mother that no one had told me about all the bizarre things that happened in a pregnancy.

I never thought you had any interest, my mother said. If I'd known, I would've told you everything!

There was a fresh intimacy when we talked, as if we were quenching an old thirst. I knew that my mother worried about the man I'd slept with; she wanted me to talk to him before long, to ask how much he would like to be involved. But she didn't want to disturb our bond, or say anything that might upset me.

It was for this reason, I assumed, that she didn't question Zoe's return to my life, either. Years ago, when I was consumed by the waning of our friendship, I had turned to my mother to vent my frustration. I told her about the time Zoe had asked for my help in writing a proposal. I'd given her all my best ideas, I said bitterly, but once Zoe received the grant, she never acknowledged my contribution. My mother had raged against Zoe, and told me that I should not trust her again. My mother generally thought of me as being naive in friendships, giving more than I received. I needed her comfort. Otherwise, I might have told her that even the most seemingly one-sided friendships worked on reciprocity; if I offered more, I also received the satisfaction of my own kindness.

Zoe and I had both got generous commissions in the past weeks. Our old competition seemed truly irrelevant now. We discussed how bountiful this time of growth was. We'd made a routine of talking on the phone in the evenings while walking.

No wonder, Zoe said, that birth and creativity spring from the same chakra. The world was opening up to us, setting us on our paths.

I, too, had begun to talk like Zoe—about intentions and fate, the deep knowledge of nature and our bodies. I liked the underlying message within this way of speaking—that everything happened for a reason, that I was at the center of meaning with my unique wisdom.

During one of our evening conversations, we decided that I would visit Zoe and her husband in their town for a long weekend. I was in my third month by then, and already feeling less tired. My trip would coincide with a gathering Zoe was organizing. Not a baby shower, she emphasized, but a ceremony to celebrate life.

WHEN IT HAPPENED—when the bleeding started—I was at home. I called my mother as soon as I got in the taxi.

Oh, no, my mother said. Oh, no no no no no.

I had called her in part thinking that she might be able to stop it, absurdly remembering the theory of the Greek school. *Calling on the protection of the community*, the man had said, and I repeated his words over and over until the taxi pulled up at the hospital.

In the emergency room, I was asked to wait. One woman was brought in on a stretcher, escorted by two policemen. When she went to the toilet to provide her urine sample, one of the policemen went with her and the other guarded the main door. Another woman arrived with a gym bag. Soon a nurse came to her side and asked if she was ready.

All right, the woman said, smiling. Let's go.

I was trying to intuit whether I was still in the other dimension, but it was so hard to tell, to untangle one thing from the other.

The doctor was kind, and matter-of-fact. He said that he didn't have good news for me. He presented the options—medicine or surgical removal—adding that I could certainly wait several days before making a decision.

It's completely up to you, he said, as if he were doing me a great favor. Whatever you'd like.

I called my mother again on my way home. Night had fallen, and I'd decided to walk back, along an avenue with a thick tunnel of trees. I couldn't speak because of my sobbing, and my mother rushed to soothe me, pleading that it would be all right. Even then, I knew that she must be in greater pain than I was. And she was charged with the task of staying strong. *Perhaps*, I thought, *this was the power of which the woman had spoken.*

For the sake of my mother, I calmed myself. I repeated to her what the doctor had told me: that it had happened some weeks ago, and there would have been no way of preventing it.

At home, I texted Zoe. I was hoping she would call me immediately, as she had the first time, because I wanted to cry without rein.

Oh, darling, Zoe wrote back. *Oh, my sweetheart.*

But she didn't call.

The next morning, I had a message that she was thinking of me, followed by a line of throbbing red hearts.

For the rest of the week, I waited for it to begin. I'd been told at the hospital that it might take some time to start on its own, and that the safest course would be to end it as soon as possible. I was prescribed three different painkillers, each one stronger than the last, so that, should I decide to take the medicine, I would feel very little. The operation would also be pain-free. I would fall asleep and wake up and it would be gone. The thought disturbed me: it was a horror to not feel anything, to force my mind to adjust to the reality that my body hadn't yet accepted. I still felt nauseous; I couldn't stand the smell of perfume or alcohol; my abdomen was swollen. Phrases that Zoe might have used came to me as possible pieces of wisdom: that my body would know what to do, that with acceptance would come relief. But I was no longer in the dimension, and these words did nothing to bring it back. Nor had I returned to the old one; I was now in a different place altogether, with its own misty depths.

During these days, I was told repeatedly that what had happened to me was very common. It was a shame, everyone said, that out of humiliation or superstition women did not talk about it more often. I was given statistics. Friends told me stories far more tragic than my own: women who'd experienced this farther along, lived through stillbirths, or the deaths of their young children. The stories didn't make me feel lucky, because they didn't mean that I had been spared. Rather, I felt that I had now entered the realm of misfortune, where tragedies suddenly became possibilities, rather than anecdotes about the lives of others.

I hadn't spoken to Zoe since she'd sent me the message of throbbing hearts, and I sensed that she was avoiding the corrupted atmosphere that surrounded me—that she feared it would be harmful for her to approach, to breathe in the fumes of my hazardous environment.

I kept remembering, then forgetting, that I should tell Zoe I would not be able to make it to her celebration that weekend, though I assumed that she would have figured this out already. I decided to go on a trip alone to the sea, and bought a train ticket for the next day, with only a hasty note to tell my boss that I would be away. I realized that I must be acting strangely, but I had no strength for explanations.

THE CONTRACTIONS BEGAN as the train left the city—traveling past the suburbs, the factories, the empty industrial allotments—then subsided as we moved through fields and small towns erupting out of the cloth of hills.

Some hours later they started again, washing over me with their own meaning so that I no longer had to think about my situation or try to make sense of it. I needed only to bear the pain. I knew that these were probably not contractions but cramps; I wasn't giving birth but disposing of life. And yet, in this dimension, they constituted their own sort of birth, a solemn ceremony.

By the morning, at the pension I had booked for the weekend, it was all over. The pain had pressed down on me in crashes of thunder, threatening to split me apart. Then—swiftly, mercifully—it had departed.

I walked on the beach, windy that day and unpopulated. The great length of sand filled me with a determination to carry on. I walked for almost an hour, then sat on a smooth bed of rock. I thought how nice it would be to have lunch and a glass of wine when I returned to the pension. The dimension was withdrawing, collapsing in on itself, just like the shocking departure from my body some hours before. I could see myself back in the world, with its simple joys and routines.

At the pension I checked my phone. There was a call from my mother, and several messages from friends, asking how I was doing. I responded to them one by one, describing the events of the morning and adding that I felt much better.

I'd inquired at the reception desk about lunch, and received an enthusiastic recommendation for a café. I would go there after a nap, the thought of which filled me with pleasure. I kicked off my shoes and got into bed. For some minutes I browsed on my phone—news sites and social media—feeling grateful that I could be interested in any of this, in the old, familiar flatness. I saw that Zoe had posted photographs from her ceremony. She was wearing the same long dress she'd worn to our lunch, and had a wreath of flowers in her hair. It was a perfect costume, communicating all the creativity and bounty that she and I used to talk about on our evening walks. Two women I didn't know stood on either side of her, with their hands on her belly.

I could see another reason for Zoe's silence, one that differed from my feeling that my misfortune repulsed her. It might simply have been awkward that what happened to me coincided with her celebration. She had decided that once she'd had a chance to honor her happiness, she would attend to me. She'd hold a space for both, she must have reasoned, the light and the dark.

It all seemed so ordinary—this bargaining with the universe.

I was sure I would receive a message from Zoe very soon, even that day, suggesting that we talk on the phone or meet up. *But only if you feel ready,* Zoe would add. The murky days were over. She could now offer me condolence and wish me strength.

The Room

"At one time," the landlord tells Leyla, leading her up the wooden staircase, "this side of the building was occupied by servants."

He turns around to look at her, to see whether she understands. Leyla nods her head.

The landlord himself, Monsieur Guerin, lives in the main building in front. The two buildings share the same entrance but are otherwise segregated. When Leyla met the landlord earlier in the hallway, she made toward the grand birdcage elevator.

"Ah, no," Monsieur Guerin said, motioning her to a back door, beyond which stood the garbage bins, and past them, a narrow staircase.

When they reach the top floor, Monsieur Guerin pauses to steady his breathing and flaps his shirt back and forth. The pocket is embroidered with his initials.

"We haven't used the room in a long time," he says as he opens the door. "My wife used to draw here, but I guess she doesn't like climbing the stairs."

The room is flooded with light. There is a sink in the corner, an old desk, a daybed fitted with patterned burgundy fabric. It's the details she loves immediately—the worn wooden floors, terra-cotta tiles beneath the sink, the single drawer of the desk with a keyhole, the bed's brass claws. From the window she sees the slanting rooftops of buildings facing the inner courtyard—exactly what she would have imagined for a life in Paris.

"We can take that out," Monsieur Guerin says, pointing at the bed. He tells her he owns another room down the corridor, a little one, for storage.

"Do you understand me?" he demands in slow, punctuated French. Leyla nods.

She tells him she doesn't mind the bed, but she doesn't say she's planning on living here. Things have changed since the days of the servants' quarters; it's no longer legal to live in such rooms. This one is advertised as a study, "at the foot of the Luxembourg Gardens, ideal for quiet, creative work." Leyla guesses now that these are Madame Guerin's words.

"That's all there is," Monsieur Guerin says. He adds that the shared toilets are down the corridor, pointing loosely with his hand, even though the top floor is mostly empty.

"I'm not sure this little place would be useful to you."

"It's exactly what I need," Leyla tells him. She asks whether she can begin using it immediately.

"All the same to me. Just an empty room."

She takes out two months' rent she's brought along, hoping to settle everything today. Monsieur Guerin tells her she can continue to pay in cash in the future.

"We'll keep it simple," he adds, as if the small amount is not worth fussing over, though it's more likely that he doesn't want to declare the loose ends of his earnings.

HER ROOMMATES ARE surprised that she would want to move out of their shared apartment, where Leyla has lived during her first months in the city. They repeat daily how lucky they are to be all together in this phase of their lives. They like to think of themselves as a community, and of the intimate time they share as indispensable to their artistic growth. Paris is still an unreal city to them all, with the elusive promise of inspiration, though it requires confirmation to believe this, when their lives can just as easily seem to be floating without direction. And for this they spend all their time together, without a moment of solitude.

It's become clear to Leyla that she wants to be alone, even if she can't afford a proper place. She's already figured out that she can shower at a nearby pool. It won't be so much trouble, she decides; it might even add something to her life here.

So much of her days are spent in other people's homes, as luxurious as they are sterile. Her students' families move in for a year or two on business contracts. The children adjust to their new international schools, identical in every country, so that they may even forget where they're living. Tutors are brought in to stitch together any difficulties. Leyla has had no trouble finding work with the credentials of her elite American education, though this doesn't prevent her from being treated as one of the nameless servants.

She often has the sense, when she goes to these apartments, that she is breaking in. Money is left for her in an envelope by the door; she's buzzed in without a word of welcome, the door left ajar for her to make her own way to students' bedrooms. She sits next to them at their desks, facing posters of celebrities, half-naked women, and race cars. Male students try flirting with her. They tell her about their vacations, show her videos of themselves snowboarding and jet-skiing.

The female students admire her composure and intelligence, what they call her magical ability to find the right words. Whenever they try to give words to their half-formed ideas, their sentences expand like chewing gum. They seek Leyla's approval, put on a show of docility, but become spoiled on a whim whenever they're frustrated. Then they roll their eyes, take out their phones.

AS THEY DESCEND the stairs, Monsieur Guerin shows her the three keys—for the room, for the servants' door, for the main entrance. When they are back in the marble hallway, he asks her how she plans to use the room.

"Writing," Leyla says.

"You're a writer?"

"Yes."

It's not out of deception that she doesn't mention tutoring, but because she doesn't think that the hours she spends going over her students' essays, sentence by illogical sentence, define her profoundly.

Her friends, too, are all invested in their proclaimed careers, which double as identities—filmmakers, artists, poets—though there is, as yet, little to show for them, while their days are spent in tedious work.

"I *want* to be a writer," she corrects herself now to Monsieur Guerin, aware that her clumsy French does not match her statement, that she must sound too childish for the landlord to believe that she is capable, and sophisticated. But Monsieur Guerin doesn't ask what language she writes in.

"And you?" she asks.

"Retired."

He doesn't say what he's retired from, which itself must be a mark of his successful past. Leyla likes this arrogance.

She can spot the signs of retirement, as if he's recently loosened his grip. His skin is lightly tanned, his gray hair swept back. The lines at the corners of his eyes fold upward each time he vaguely smiles at her. It's not a full smile, certainly not familiar, but enough to be polite.

"I hope the room serves your needs," he says and hands her the keys.

After they part, Leyla walks to the gardens, mostly empty except for elderly couples sitting with their eyes closed, facing the sun. A few tourists have set up picnics on benches, with rosé wine and cheese, though it's hardly the season, in autumn. *This is her neighborhood now*, Leyla thinks, *where other people come on holiday.*

SHE SPENDS HER mornings reading, or looking out the window. She can see rooftops and inside some apartments. A kitchen sink; an old woman watering flowers; a man at his desk. So many quiet lives. Some days she sits for hours on her bed, doing nothing. She doesn't think that she is doing nothing, or rather, she doesn't ask herself what she's doing. She lets her mind drift, then settle into blankness, seeping out toward the corners and the walls.

The bed, the desk, the floorboards and tiles have taken on the texture of her days. Each evening after lesson, when she steps in through the door, she feels the room taking her in and sealing behind her. She has the sense, every time she's back, that she and the room are picking things up where they left off, continuing their time together. She has bought a creeping plant with yellow-green leaves that unfurl at surprising speed, the vines inching down the desk to the floor, toward the window.

In the afternoons she walks to the swimming pool, tiled with tiny blue-and-green mosaics. She doesn't count her laps, and comes out of the water when she feels her muscles gently throbbing. She swims for an hour, sometimes longer, before she showers and goes to her students' homes to teach in the evenings.

She has begun to love this routine, as she does the neighborhood, her side of the building, her room. From the outside, her living arrangement might seem awkward, a half-life. She eats canned sardines and crackers sitting on the bed, she heats beans with the help of an electric kettle. Each morning, she retrieves clothes from two suitcases underneath the bed. But what matters to her is that she feels welcomed in her own life, and free. She is surprised that it's been this simple—making herself useful enough to be paid; living in a beautiful place where she can close the door and be alone.

She thinks that in time, she will write here. But there is no rush, unlike for her friends, who always talk of another life, brighter and more established than their own. They are impatient to be rid of the modest jobs they consider embarrassments, even humiliations.

Recently, barely fifteen minutes into a lesson, a mother came to the bedroom and told Leyla she would have to leave.

"We're going out early," she said. "Sweetheart, why don't you get ready?"

Then she added to Leyla, "Don't worry, we'll pay you anyway."

But humiliation requires participation, and Leyla pretends not to hear her.

DURING THEIR GATHERINGS on the riverbanks, in dim wine bars, warehouses converted to cafés, she joins her friends' conversations about their inspirations and readings, the artists who've achieved what they wish to do. These conversations are themselves a consolation; the listing of names a sort of spell that affirms their passions.

"What're you working on?" they ask each other, every time. And with that they're carried away recounting their unrealized projects, unpacking the minutest moments of their consciousness into creative possibility.

But Leyla doesn't want to be swept away from her life, from the room where her thoughts have only just begun to settle.

·

AFTER THE FIRST month, Monsieur Guerin sends her a text message suggesting several half-hour slots in the late afternoon when she can go over to pay the rent. They agree on a weekend morning. Leyla takes the birdcage elevator to the top floor. The smell here is entirely different—all brass and marble and airiness, unlike the musty wood of her side.

Once again, Monsieur Guerin is impeccably dressed in a shirt and pressed trousers. He asks Leyla to step inside, but doesn't invite her any further. The walls of the long corridor are covered with art, testament to their owners' extensive tastes. There are old maps, abstract oil paintings, embroidered fabrics. Beyond the hallway is the living room with arched windows overlooking the chestnut trees in the gardens.

Madame Guerin appears from a back room. She's dressed in matching light colors; her hair swirls inward at her chin. She has her husband's confident attitude as she assesses Leyla in one glance. But age has taken a different expression with her. She is puckered, almost embittered by the folds of her skin, unlike Monsieur Guerin, who looks out at the world with conviction.

"My husband tells me you're a writer." Madame Guerin says. "I used to draw in that room. It's perfect for inspiration, don't you think?"

"Are you an artist?" Leyla asks.

"Not really," she says. Leyla notices something like an apology in her look.

"Well, is everything all right with the room?" Monsieur Guerin says.

Leyla follows his cue to leave—she does not want to appear nosy, or wait to be invited inside. She hands him the envelope, wishes them a good weekend. Madame Guerin tells her that next time she should come in for tea.

SOME AFTERNOONS ON her way to the pool, Leyla sees Madame Guerin walking in the gardens. She often walks with another woman her age, both of them dressed for sports, though they walk at a leisurely pace. There is that same look of apology whenever Madame Guerin sees her, seeping through her confidence.

She has twice seen Monsieur Guerin as well, walking alone in the early morning. His pace was swift, and he didn't notice her because both times he was talking on the phone, with a full smile on his face, almost a grin, utterly unlike the reined-in smile when he speaks to Leyla.

"I saw you in the gardens," she tells him the next time she pays the rent. "You're lucky to live so close by. I love going there, too, for inspiration."

She is surprised at herself for the effort she's making. Perhaps she wants to prove to Monsieur Guerin that she has a fuller life than her awkward French suggests. She's aware that she wants him to like her.

"Yes," Monsieur Guerin says. "It's good to start the day with exercise."

He takes the envelope, wishes her a good day. He closes the door without waiting for her elevator to arrive.

LEYLA IS HIRED to tutor a high schooler for two hours every day. She won't have any free time in the evenings, but she will make a good amount of money.

The apartment overlooks the gilded dome of Les Invalides and the riding tracks of the military school. Leyla proposes working in the dining room, facing the view.

"Big deal," the girl says. "I see it all the time."

"I don't," Leyla says. "And it's a shame to let it go to waste."

The girl has failed her midterm English exam and hasn't read any of the poems for the new unit. It's likely, her teacher has informed the parents, that she will fail the class at the end of the semester. The mother tells Leyla they don't expect her to perform miracles.

"Anything you manage is a plus," she says. "At this point, we've given up."

When they sit down, facing the view, Leyla asks the girl whether she likes poetry.

"*No?*" the girl says. "Does *anyone?*"

For the remainder of their time together, she doodles swirling vines all along the sides of her notebook.

The following evening, Leyla brings a poem about a bird. She tells the girl she doesn't care whether she understands the poem. What she wants is for her to draw lines that represent the poem's sounds.

"What do you mean?" the girl says.

"Imagine that you don't speak English, and you're drawing what it sounds like."

The girl sits, sullen, through the first reading. Then, as Leyla reads the poem a second time, she picks up her pen and makes short, staccato diagonals on the page. On the third reading, she adds long swoops that twist and turn into infinity signs. She follows the poem's alliterations with her pen, dotting along the page.

"Look," Leyla tells her, following the marks on the page with her finger. "You've drawn the flight of a bird."

Later, when they're reading a poem assigned for class, and the girl is once again frustrated, Leyla tells her to forget about the meaning and find a few words that sound nice to her.

"I have no idea what you mean," the girl says.

"I'm just asking you to pick out whatever you find beautiful. Do you ever have trouble picking out a dress you like?"

The girl rolls her eyes, but she does spot a few words that, she says, sound all right.

Voyaging cloudlike and unpent . . .

"I don't even know what that means," she adds, and Leyla tells her it doesn't matter.

EACH MONTH, SHE messages with Monsieur Guerin about the rent. He is unaccommodating in his schedule, and responds to Leyla's messages with a curt *No, sorry* if the time doesn't suit him.

One Saturday evening they agree that she will pay the rent on Monday. Hours later, Leyla remembers that the bank is closed on Mondays and writes back to tell Monsieur Guerin.

I can come on Tuesday or Wednesday, she texts. *Any time that works for you.* She is never sure of her grammar, the accent marks, the additional *e* that follows certain verbs if employed by a woman. But she assumes Monsieur Guerin will understand what she means, and she doesn't bother checking her spelling.

He texts back immediately, as if they had been chatting all along, even though it usually takes him several hours to write back to her. His message confuses Leyla.

and any accessories you'd like . . . !!

When she understands what has happened, she is surprised most of all by his punctuation—the suggestive imagination of the ellipses, the enthusiasm of the double exclamation, so unlike the matter-of-fact man she knows.

Immediately, another message follows.

. . . like that time in the room!

Leyla puts her phone away. Later that night, she sees that Monsieur Guerin has sent another text, this time in the character that she knows.

Apologies. Wrong person.

She doesn't respond, and on Monday she doesn't contact him to arrange another time to pay the rent. She feels uncomfortable about what she has unwittingly glimpsed, even if this is Monsieur Guerin's business, and she cannot be one to judge.

Leyla wonders whether his mistake has anything to do with her clumsy French; whether the room in the message is her own, or the little storage Monsieur Guerin mentioned. It's not unlikely that such a man would have a lover, and it's easy enough to imagine that he used the room for this purpose before Leyla moved in—the most convenient for himself, instead of a more sophisticated arrangement. Perhaps it was his wife who put the room up for rent, feeling suspicious.

Leyla imagines that Monsieur Guerin will be composed the next time she sees him. He will certainly not bring up his mistake. He is the type of person who would find it distasteful to make a scandal of someone's private business. She can picture handing him the envelope in the hallway. He will ask her whether all is well with the room, without really waiting for an answer, then close the door behind her. The thought of this upsets her. She is angered by his imaginary composure, his self-righteousness. She decides she will wait for him to contact her.

That month, Leyla doesn't pay the rent. By the following month, there is still no news from Monsieur Guerin, and Leyla supposes that at this point he probably won't ask her to settle for the past month. They will simply proceed as if nothing has happened.

She uses the extra money to cut back on work. She ends her lessons with her new student, which take up all her evenings. Leyla feels a bit sorry to leave her; the girl got a passing grade on her last homework, and she looks forward to their sessions, even though she tries to hide it. With time and some effort, Leyla might even have inspired the girl. She writes her a note of encouragement. She hopes that she will continue to read poetry, she says, and to notice beauty in all things.

THE STORY OF her landlord is an ongoing topic of discussion among her friends. They imagine what Monsieur Guerin's lover might be like, and Leyla describes to them the fine balance of Monsieur Guerin's old age and charm. It's neither a profound love affair, they guess, nor purely professional, but something in between. They laugh at what must have been Guerin's shock at realizing that he sent the message to his young tenant.

"Gaping Guerin," one of them says, and the name sticks. They tell Leyla she could probably blackmail him and not pay rent for the rest of the year.

"Don't be ridiculous," Leyla says, even though she has made no attempt to contact her landlord since the message.

ONE MORNING, AS she's coming out of the building, she sees Madame Guerin coming back home in her matching sports clothes. Leyla pretends not to see her and crosses the street, but the woman calls after her.

"I missed you the other day," Madame Guerin says.

Leyla is confused; she doesn't respond.

"My husband said you came by when I was out."

"You should come for tea," Madame Guerin adds. "We want to hear about your writing."

Leyla tells her that she'll let them know. They walk together up to the end of the street, and both turn left toward the boulevard.

"Is there anything you need for the room?" Madame Guerin asks.

Leyla shakes her head.

"I probably have an electric burner," Madame Guerin says. "If you wanted to cook up there."

She smiles sweetly and allows a moment to pass, as if to say she knows Leyla's secret.

"Thank you," Leyla says. "I don't need anything."

"What a shame I never made anything of that room for years. You should use it well."

Leyla nods her head. She doesn't know why she can't bring herself to offer any sympathy, or friendship.

They part at the next road.

In the afternoon, she's back in her room and doesn't have to leave again to teach. She sits on the bed, thinking of a story about a young man who lives in a similar room, watching the lives of his neighbors. She has the image of a hand closing a door; solitude contrasted with lives unraveling all around. But she cannot quite see how any of this might fit into the story, how she would give it form and meaning.

When it grows dark, she gets up to tidy the room, sorting through a pile on her bed. Then she clears the desk.

She's relieved that she won't have to worry about hearing from Monsieur Guerin that month, and she decides for certain that she won't do anything until he contacts her. He's told his wife that Leyla has already paid, which makes her believe she can take advantage of the situation without getting in trouble. She thinks vaguely that she has every right to do this, even if Monsieur Guerin is relying on her participation to cover things up. *He is*, Leyla thinks for a fleeting moment, *making her an offer of complicity*. But she tells herself, once again, that it's her right to let the month pass; that she will use the extra time to start writing something.

The Room

The apartments across the courtyard are lighting up. Two children wash their hands together at the kitchen sink.

She turns on the light, and the room is illuminated dramatically, with large shadows on the yellow-tinted walls. Finally, she sits down at the desk and tries collecting her thoughts so she can begin.

Outside, the last light of the evening disappears. And it seems that her room is getting smaller.

We Are Here

Summer vanished. All along the Volga, the beer tents where we'd gathered our first weeks were folded up and put into trucks. For a few days the town's students sat among the poles. By the following week the poles were stacked and carried away, and the boardwalk looked empty on the gray water.

Trees turned their leaves and shed them, like the peeling paint of the town's yellow buildings. Majestic round hats appeared with the first sharp wind sweeping in from the river. It was a sight we'd always imagined. The fur coats, too. Cafés were lit neon at daytime. Solitary drunks sat in the empty park. Old women bundled in felt and wool sold vegetables out of buckets.

Finally, we had a sense of where we'd come. And we were gladdened by the gloom.

We wished for things to get darker, and colder. We wished for snow, for the gray light. We almost cheered at the unsmiling waitresses, hoped they would ignore us for longer, shrug when we asked them in our comical accents whether they had the *pelmeni*. We would look at each other, then, smiling triumphantly.

"Welcome to Russia," we'd say.

Back at university, our dorm rooms were decorated with Soviet-era posters of women workers, advertisements for chocolate with the face of the freckled boy Kuzya, cartoon characters we hadn't grown up with. We were nostalgic for these things that didn't belong to us. We were born several decades too late; we longed for things that were more real, a little decrepit.

One of us had set out to read *The Master and Margarita* in Russian, another *War and Peace*. We stated our goals without hesitation our first year at university, while we struggled to conjugate the genitive case. We said we had always been drawn to this culture and its people, and we used words like *stoic* and *noble* to describe our passion.

THERE WERE A few other foreigners in town. We met them at the internet café where all the foreigners gathered daily. A German businessman who'd lived for a year in Delaware took all of us out to dinner our first week, when we were up for doing anything. We would meet after class to go to the market and try the foods that looked the strangest; we went to a sauna even before the weather was cold.

"You guys are great," the businessman told us at dinner. He ordered us shots. "You remind me of my student years."

Afterward, when we stood shivering outside, coughing on cigarettes, he said, "Welcome to Russia, everyone. It's a lot of fun here." We didn't see him again.

There were the two missionary boys, or that's what we guessed they were, because their good looks didn't match their bashful ways. They were bewildered by our jokes. And there were the Italian girls who'd come to work in an orphanage.

We would all meet up at KFC, perhaps only to make a point of our displacement, feeling kinship as we ate potato wedges.

"Finally, something without sour cream," we said. "Something that's not pickled."

Every morning in class we told each other what our host families had prepared for dinner. Smoked eel, cabbage of a hundred varieties, pancakes with cottage cheese. For some reason, all this made us roar with laughter. We exchanged stories of our hosts in a sort of competition, observing everything they did like comedians. One of us slept on a foldout couch in the kitchen. One suspected that the "uncle" who visited the family weekly, while the father was away in Switzerland, was actually the mother's lover. These were the stories we would share when we were back the following year, and in telling them to each other, we made them legitimate—the story of this baffling world that we had seen. A story of our experience.

Before I arrived, I imagined giving myself up to this time like entering a cocoon. I would emerge from it a year later, transformed into a better version of myself. I trusted that the year would fill me with all the things I lacked without even knowing what they were.

I lived with Galina Ivanovna, whose brightly dyed orange hair matched the tiny flowers on her cotton dresses. She walked up and down the corridor all day, sorting a growing hive of plastic bags hanging from the radiator knob, putting away leftovers in the refrigerator or on the balcony, then changing their places for no apparent reason. I guessed that she was in her eighties, but people looked older than their years. (We called this the Russki metamorphosis—all the thin blond girls transforming overnight into babushkas.)

Galina Ivanovna lived downtown, close to the university where we had our classes. Her stone building had arched windows and an impressive door, rounded and rusty. She told me proudly that a movie had once been filmed in this building. Inside, it smelled of mold. The apartment itself was very old, its leaking pipes and cracks secured by a system of rubber bands, cardboard, and cotton.

I slept in the living room on the divan, by a glass cabinet stacked with a blue china dining set and crystal glasses. Next to them I placed my contact solution and creams.

At breakfast and at dinner we sat across the kitchen table on two stools, and Galina Ivanovna asked me, "Soup, now? Chicken, now?"

She served the dishes one by one, regardless of my answer.

From the moment that I introduced myself, she swept my name aside and called me Masha.

"It's just you and me, Masha," she said on our first dinner of soup and pancakes.

Her sister Irina, who had lived upstairs, had recently passed away. Irina had been a host mother, too, up until the very end. Irina's two children lived in Moscow.

"And your children?"

She shook her head.

"But you like students?" I asked.

Galina Ivanovna got up from the table. After a few minutes, she came back with a photo album and pulled her stool next to mine. She started on the first page and showed me, one by one, the photographs of girls in college sweatshirts and cable-knit sweaters, smiling brightly in front of the glass cabinet.

"Sasha, Alya, Lara," she said. "Tanya, Katya."

There were also photos of the girls hugging Galina Ivanovna or holding her hand. She waved her hand in the air as if to dismiss them, as if she were embarrassed, but she did not rush to flip the page. At the end of the album were several photographs sent from the United States, of Christmas gatherings, hiking trips, the Disneyland castle.

"This is Florida," Galina Ivanovna said. "This is Maine." She took the pictures out of the plastic sheet to show me the place names written in Cyrillic on the back. It was clear that these girls, who had shared something of their own lives with her, were Galina Ivanovna's favorites, and she remembered them by their real names.

"My Jessica," she said. "Look, beautiful Stephanie."

The following evening, while we sat at the kitchen after dinner, she asked whether I would like to go to the theater. She could ask her friend, who worked at the ticket booth, to get us in.

"Thank you," I said. "That's OK."

I tried to explain that I wouldn't understand a play in Russian.

"Concert?" Galina Ivanovna asked.

"That's OK," I said again. "Thank you very much."

I was planning on joining the others after class to go to KFC.

"Irina loves the theater," she said, and I wondered whether she was speaking in the present tense for my sake.

"I wish I'd known her," I said.

"Won't you be bored here, doing nothing?"

I opened my hands in the form of a book. I pantomimed writing.

After a while Galina Ivanovna said, "Everyone's gone."

I nodded my head. Then I said, "I'm here. You're here."

After we'd cleared the table, she followed me to the living room and took out a frame from the back of the glass cabinet. She pointed at the photograph of a man with a mustache, wearing army medals.

"My husband," she said. "He also travels. He reads a lot, like you girls."

Next day in class I told the others that my host mother was a real character.

"Guys," I said, "I think she communes with the dead."

BY NOVEMBER THE trees were barren. We had done everything there was to do in town. We'd visited the cathedral, walked the boardwalk to the medieval fortress, gone mushroom picking with one of the hosts, gone to the discotheque. We even went to a play and left after the first act. We visited the Italian girls at the orphanage and spent an afternoon drawing with the children. We took a weekend trip to Tolstoy's estate, where we bought fur hats and flower-patterned shawls like the old women wore at the market.

When I came home from the trip, my shawl draped in a triangle on my back, Galina Ivanovna took me by the arm to her room and sat me on the bed.

She brought down a cloth-bound bundle from the wardrobe and untied it on the floor.

"My mother," she said, holding up a camisole. And she said it again, showing me a tablecloth, its matching napkins, a crepe dress. I pantomimed sewing with my hands, and she nodded.

"My mother," she said.

At the bottom, there was a pair of baby's socks, and a tiny blue-checkered dress.

That evening Galina Ivanovna asked me to sit with her in her room to watch a show about a girl in high school, with thick glasses and braces. We had tea, and Galina Ivanovna went to her wardrobe and brought out a bag of sweets.

When the show started, she pointed at the dark-haired actor.

"She likes him," she informed me. "But he doesn't pay her attention."

I guessed that the heroine would undergo some sort of transformation in the coming episodes, as they all did. I got up during the commercial break, forming my hands into a pillow next to my cheek.

"All right, then," Galina Ivanovna said, and waved me off.

I lay on the divan and finished the grammar exercises for the following day. I added some details to the paragraph describing my hometown. I wrote that there were large maple trees, famous for their autumn colors; that my family members all lived close by; that even though it was small, it was a beautiful town. I tried to use all the words

I knew in Russian, but the accumulation did not resemble my home: post office, library, park, bench, pool, cinema.

Afterward I took out my journal, where I recorded details each evening—the smell of beets in the apartment; the square pieces of newspaper cut up to use as toilet paper. I added the bundle of old clothes Galina Ivanovna had shown me, and the bag of stale candy in her wardrobe.

THERE WAS THE boredom we exaggerated—*Damn, this town's boring*—and there was boredom itself.

Every evening after class, I walked the few blocks to Galina Ivanovna's building, then walked back to the university to do my homework in a classroom. Afterward I'd wander around town, ending up by the cathedral. The others would have gone to their host families. They all lived in the suburbs and were worried about getting back in the evening when buses were less frequent. I was lucky to be living in the center, with the freedom to come and go as I pleased. The others said there was nothing at all around their neighborhoods—neither a shop nor a park, just the dreary concrete blocks side by side along the road. Once they were home, they told me, they were more or less imprisoned. Perhaps this was why they began participating in their families' lives. They babysat for the children, visited acquaintances, helped prepare time-consuming traditional dishes. As they settled into their routines, I thought that I was the unlucky one, after all, that I was missing out on an authentic experience.

In the evenings I lay on the divan, contemplating whether I had anything else to add to my journal. I'd already described the town, as well as some historical facts and legends. I copied poems from *Doctor Zhivago* that I'd brought with me for inspiration.

After her TV show was over, Galina Ivanovna would come to the living room and sit on the edge of the divan. She would tell me what we would have for breakfast, and for dinner, and when I confirmed, she would say, "In that case, I'll go to the market tomorrow."

I thought that perhaps this was her way of asking whether I wanted to join her.

Sometimes, while she chatted, she would begin unbuttoning her dress without the slightest sign of discomfort. She wore layers of clothes beneath—a cotton shirt tucked into her underpants, long socks—so that she was never really naked. Still, I was so surprised the first time this happened that I got up and went to the cabinet to take off my contacts. Galina Ivanovna took off her dress and draped it on her knees. I asked her if she was preparing to go to sleep.

"Don't worry about it," she said, as if I'd offered to help her around the apartment, so she could go to bed quickly. "I just have a few things to finish up."

I was amused to think of all the ways I could recount the situation to the others. But the period of competing for our hosts' eccentricities had already passed.

AT THE END of November a box arrived from one of the students' parents, filled with Snickers bars, sour candy, popcorn, and an abundant assortment of books. The parent must have been told that we had exhausted our entire reading stock as well as that of the town's bookstore, which had three books in English—*The Picture of Dorian Gray, Little Women, The Call of the Wild*. In the box there were thrillers, spy novels, current bestsellers back home, books about exotic places—Kabul, Shanghai, Saint Petersburg—about revolutionaries or seamstresses.

We divided the books among us and exchanged them regularly. I read faster than the others and urged them to finish their books quickly. Some gave them to me without reading until the end. They were comfortable in their routines by then. I observed the change—their calmness, the gradual ebbing away of their bewilderment at this new life.

I read without rationing, going to the living room as soon as I got home, without giving Galina Ivanovna the chance to come and tell me about her day. We had also settled into a routine, moving about the apartment without disturbing each other. I left home before breakfast and read in an empty classroom. I joined Galina Ivanovna for dinner, getting up to wash my plate as soon as I was done, despite her protests for me to leave it in the sink. Then I went to the living room to read.

The characters and geographies blended together, the eerie and the familiar, tragedy and joy. I was happy to discover my capacity for concentration, for reading whatever came my way, as if this were proof of passion. As if here, finally, was the gleam of my transformation.

THE OTHERS WERE adopted into the social circles of their host brothers or sisters. Some of them took on hobbies—wood painting, iconography, singing with the local choir. One girl started a softball team made up of the Russian students at the university and coached them in the evenings. We helped her organize a bake sale to buy team shirts, and all the students and professors showed up, delighted by the cause. Another girl gave English classes at the orphanage.

The program coordinator told us that we were an exemplary group. We had adapted so well and quickly. There had only been one unfortunate event, when a student got mugged late one night, going home from the discotheque with his host brother. Our university sent emails of sympathy and warning, but we understood that this was the type of thing that might have happened anywhere.

•

ON THE FIRST night of snow, I decided to go for a walk. Galina Ivanovna came to the door as I was putting on my boots and told me it was too cold to be out.

"Sit with me and watch the show," she said. She smiled like a girl and reached to hold my arm. "Masha, why do you always want to be alone?"

I told her that I couldn't really follow what was going on in the show.

"Nonsense," she said. "Look how you speak."

I had my keys with me, I told her. She shouldn't worry about going to sleep.

I walked past the university and the park to the cathedral. Snowflakes flurried silently in the light cast by streetlamps. The plaza was empty. I took one of the roads leading out like rays from the cathedral—this was a unique feature of medieval city planning that I'd included in my journal. I came to the river, frozen in thin patches.

I walked toward the fortress. On the other shore, the town petered out and gave way to a dark wall of trees. I was thinking of lines I might add to my journal, trying to recall the sight of the empty plaza filling with snow, when I heard a voice behind me, telling me to be careful.

A guy, around my age, stood a few meters away, smoking a cigarette. He smiled vaguely. I nodded my head.

"Be careful," he said again. "You're going to freeze."

I didn't know whether his words were menacing or friendly, and I shrugged.

"What're you doing here, anyway?" he said. He stepped closer. I thought that he looked familiar. "Are you a poet or something?"

"No," I said. I started walking back in the direction of the cathedral and heard him laughing behind me.

"Hey," he shouted. "What's up?"

For some reason, even though I felt no danger, I walked faster with each step. Once I reached the cathedral I began to run. At home, I noticed that the money rolled up in my coat pocket had fallen out.

The following morning after class, I asked for a meeting with the coordinator and told her that I, too, had been mugged the previous evening.

"Nothing serious," I added. "No real loss."

But I told her I'd decided to return home, instead of staying on for the spring semester. The coordinator said I shouldn't rush to a decision. It would be a shame to go back now, just as I was getting comfortable in Russian. I agreed with her, nodding the entire time that she spoke.

"When else will you get such an opportunity?" she asked.

I added that there was, in fact, another issue: I didn't have much opportunity, as it were, to speak Russian with my host. She was too old, I said, and I wasn't sure that she was entirely capable of hosting a student at her age. I alluded to the fact that besides her physical limitations, she was perhaps not mentally capable, either—she could not clearly distinguish between the living and the dead and she had, on several occasions, taken off her clothes in front of me.

The coordinator was alarmed.

"We didn't know about this," she said. "All the girls have always loved her."

She offered to find me another family.

Galina Ivanovna was a wonderful woman, I agreed. But it was no one's fault that she was getting old.

I added that it might be better for me to concentrate on academics the following semester, anyway. Russian was not even my major.

The coordinator urged me to stay at least through the holidays. I could see that she was concerned, as much for me as for the reputation of the program.

"All right," I said. "And thank you for everything."

Before leaving her office, I told her Galina Ivanovna was very sensitive. It would be best not to mention what I'd said.

SOME WERE SPENDING the holidays with their hosts. Others were traveling to Moscow. I decided to join them, and would go on another trip from there, perhaps to Kazan, or north to Arkhangelsk—I had in mind a train journey ending in a fabled, mythical place before my return home.

During my last weeks in town, I went to class eagerly, made decks of vocabulary cards, filled my journal with all the sights and sounds I encountered. I attended choir practice, went to the orphanage for a day of games with the children. When I came home, Galina Ivanovna would tell me that she had left me food on the table, just in case.

"Masha, did I do something wrong?" she asked one morning as I was leaving. After class, I told her, I was going to one of the other host's for dinner.

"No," I said. "I just want to make the most of my time before I leave."

"You're leaving because you don't like it here?"

"I like it," I mumbled.

I couldn't think of anything else to say.

ONE DAY BEFORE the trip to Moscow, I got sick. By the following morning, when the others were boarding the train, I was so ill that I couldn't stand up.

Galina Ivanovna came to the living room every hour, holding her hand to my forehead, changing my pillowcase, bringing soup that I didn't touch.

"Come on, Mashenka," she said. "Just a little bit."

Whenever she urged me to eat, I cried meekly, feeling pathetic.

One afternoon, when I had managed to eat a few spoonfuls, she carried my stack of books to the divan. I shook my head, no, then I thanked her.

"You love reading," she said, and this, too, made me cry.

She brought the stool from the kitchen and sat in the living room for the rest of the day. I would fall asleep and wake up, and Galina Ivanovna would be sitting on the stool, her hands on her lap, without a hint of impatience.

"You'll get sick, too," I told her. "Please don't wait here."

She waved her hand.

The next day, I rose from the divan and showered. That evening, we sat at the kitchen table. Afterward I joined Galina Ivanovna in her room to watch the show. The heroine still wore braces and thick glasses, but she had made a place for herself in the social life of the classroom. Even the dark-haired boy took notice of her.

When I was going back to the living room, Galina Ivanovna asked me what I was planning to do the following evening, New Year's Eve.

"Nothing," I told her.

"We'll eat together," she said. "It's important to be together."

In the afternoon I walked to the cathedral, its walls rising out of the snow, the gilded domes dappled white. I bought presents to take home from the wooden booths set up around the plaza. A tour guide was explaining the structure of the roads extending from the cathedral. I went inside to light a candle. Before leaving, I looked up at the lavish rows of icons, their hands raised in blessing or testimony, and I tried to distill something of this sight to take back with me. Then I went to the supermarket and bought an ice-cream cake.

Galina Ivanovna had brought the kitchen table to the living room and set it with a red cloth and crystal glasses. On a small table were appetizers and a bottle of cognac. The photograph of her husband was also on the table, and another photograph of a baby, bundled in a knitted blanket.

We raised our glasses to the coming year. Galina Ivanovna nodded at the photographs before taking a sip.

As we were clearing the table, I thanked her for hosting me and gave her a heart-shaped amber brooch I'd bought that day at the plaza.

By the time the television was showing fireworks from the Red Square, she was asleep on the divan.

LATER, I RECOUNTED her with fondness. I described her pickles and soups, her cotton print dresses, her slowly disintegrating mind, as if she were a character from a fairy tale. I said that the old woman had called me Masha and that for a time afterward I'd written to her, signing my foreign name as she had given it to me. I had even sent her a photo album—my dorm room, the dining hall, my parents' home, the streets and parks of my town, the white wooden church on the hill. On the phone, she told me that my town looked just like her own.

"You must have felt at home here," she said.

The last time I talked to her was on a New Year's Eve, not long before her death.

"Happy New Year!" I shouted. "I hope you're having a glass of cognac!"

"Remember, Masha, when you and I celebrated?"

"Of course, it was wonderful."

"You were the last. They said I shouldn't host anymore."

"You were a very good host," I said.

"You shouldn't have told them," she said. "Whatever you told them."

Then she added, "But I forgive you."

IN TELLING THE story of my Russian adventure, I would say that these months with my old host were a formative time in my life and had taught me something of the lives of others.

But of all the details I didn't include in the story, one that I still remembered was the afternoon when Galina Ivanovna brought me the stack of books. For a reason I couldn't quite understand, the sight of those books had made me cry.

Galina Ivanovna had sat on a stool by the divan and rubbed my hand between her palms. I saw that she was crying, too.

"It's so sad," I thought she said to me. I wasn't sure whether I understood her correctly.

"I'm not sad," I said. "It's OK."

She shook her head.

"We are here," she said. "Side by side."

And she told me she was sorry, because she couldn't do anything else to help.

Marseille

For her birthday, Amina asked to go on a trip. Her husband had traveled for work the previous month, and, although that wasn't exactly for pleasure, it was now understood that anything which freed either of them from child care could be considered some type of holiday. Besides, they were trying to allow each other leisurely activities—evenings out, morning runs, a movie from time to time. And, recently, nights away. They wanted to find ways of easing back into their life, which had been on hold since the baby was born.

It was so simple to slip into that old self, free of obligations; the exchange happened so naturally. Amina was already bored in the half hour she had to wait at the train station in Lyon, even though such time was hard to come by. She bought a coffee and a pack of biscuits, then sat on a bench, scrolling restlessly on her phone. Though this was her first trip away from the baby, who had recently turned one, it didn't really feel momentous. It felt, rather, as if she were putting on a coat she hadn't worn in a long time, whose shape and texture she remembered immediately.

She was going to Marseille to meet her university friends Alba and Lisa, with whom she had studied in England. They were traveling from Madrid and Zurich and would arrive at the rental apartment at around the same time as Amina. It was Lisa who'd arranged everything—set the dates, booked an apartment, compiled a list of restaurants and neighborhoods they should go to. Amina and Alba had reverted to their old joke that Lisa was their travel agent; she'd account for their hours of sleep, for every minute in the bathroom.

Amina sent her friends a photo of herself making an excited face on the platform.

Eeeee, Alba responded. Lisa sent instructions for retrieving the keys, in case the others arrived before she did.

On the train, Amina sat next to a woman traveling alone with her baby, who was refusing to nap despite the mother's frenzied attempts. Amina looked up from her reading now and then to offer the woman understanding smiles, meant to signal that she felt for her, that she didn't mind the baby's crying, but from the woman's perspective she must have appeared smug, with her book and coffee.

Amina hadn't seen her friends since her pregnancy. They used to visit regularly after Amina and her husband moved to Lyon seven years ago, to the neighborhood where Amina's husband had grown up. Amina always looked forward to these reunions; she was allowed to be a tourist with her friends, speaking too-loud English, getting a little hysterical. But Lisa and Alba were exceptionally busy in the months after the birth. This was what they'd said, when they apologized for not yet having met the baby. Their weekends were booked for months ahead. Amina had barely left the confines of her neighborhood that year, and she had thought with some bitterness that Alba and Lisa didn't know what real busyness meant. But she hadn't insisted they come. For one, she was exhausted. And their friendship had always operated in leisure: long meals, afternoon drinks, dressing up to go dancing. Amina wanted to see them on these same terms, rather than be disappointed by interrupted conversations and her friends' possible lack of interest in her daughter. She herself had never paid attention to friends' babies before; she surveyed only the mothers. She noted the physical changes, their waning interests, trying to project what might become of her in the future were she to have a child.

Next to her on the train, the baby had finally fallen asleep. The mother looked at once defeated and serene, her face sagging with fatigue. Amina considered telling the woman that this was her first trip away from her daughter, but she decided against it. She retrieved Lisa's list of restaurants and checked them one by one, already feeling that there wouldn't be enough time.

THE APARTMENT WAS a half-hour walk from the station. Amina had planned on taking a taxi, but it was so sunny when she stepped out of the train and onto the wide marble terrace that she could not bear to waste the bright day. The city lay beneath her, past a long descent of stairs. She took another selfie at the bottom, for no one in particular, because she was feeling giddy. Then she walked, dragging her suitcase, stopping from time to time to take pictures of shop fronts, the boulevard lined with palm trees.

When she entered the building, she heard Alba and Lisa exclaiming from an upper floor. She called their names, and they ran out to peer at her over the banister, all three of them shrieking.

"Let the festivities begin," Alba announced, taking Amina's bag at the door to the apartment. Lisa and Alba had already opened theirs on the living room floor. The couch was strewn with clothes—too many for the two nights they would be spending together.

"We should get going soon," Lisa said, showing Amina the route she'd mapped for the evening—drinks, dinner, a walk along the sea.

"Amazing," Amina said. "I can leave right away." She was wearing jeans and a button-down shirt, slightly stained from the baby's bottle that morning.

"Leave like this?" Alba had taken off her trousers. She was picking up clothes and putting them down without trying anything on. "It's our first evening out. I might meet someone fabulous."

Alba had separated from her boyfriend some months ago. She'd informed Amina and Lisa briefly of the fact, brushing away the details, as she did with every breakup. She'd known from the start it was just a fling, she'd texted their group chat, though Amina seemed to remember that there'd once been talk of having a child. She could no longer recall whether this had been a serious plan or simply a consequence of Alba's age, at which the question could no longer be ignored. If, that is, Alba even wanted to have a child—she'd always been at once transparent and mysterious about her desires. Blunt and elusive.

Lisa had taken off her shirt. She was not wearing a bra, and Amina thought that her body had not changed very much since their student years. Then, too, the three of them would gather in one another's rooms and invent reasons to take off their clothes. Had it been a requisite for intimacy? Or a silent competition? Full-moon gatherings and menstrual rituals—they loved that sort of thing, the way it made them beautiful, brought them together. Amina had other close friends—studious types, with whom the body became invisible, or irrelevant. It was with them that she discussed serious matters: choices, strategies, philosophies. It was with them that she could be sad. Whereas her friendship with Alba and Lisa demanded cheer; it was carried forth by a constant desire to enjoy life.

Alba and Lisa were still without clothes, showing each other tasteful, expensive options for outfits, so different from the flowery, tattered garments they'd worn as young women, when they borrowed dresses and shoes from one another for parties. Just like their clothes, her friends' bodies had more purpose now, Amina thought; they were muscled and smooth, made to look that way through discipline and deliberation. She turned away, as if she could no longer examine them on equal footing. It seemed that she'd stepped off the imaginary stage where the three of them had once stood together.

Finally, they left the apartment. Alba had settled on a short, neon-colored dress, as cheeky as it was seductive. Lisa was wearing a striped shirt and canvas trousers, identical to the neat outfit she'd just changed out of. Amina put on earrings and lipstick, surprised how these small adjustments brought her into her body. Lisa led the way, phone in hand, through several small streets and out onto a wide boulevard, crowded even as shops were closing.

It was so nice, Lisa said, to be in a city that was alive.

"Zurich makes me feel old," she said, when they'd arrived at a rooftop bar overlooking the harbor, bustling with tattooed and pierced people. Her boyfriend didn't mind the monotony of the city, whereas she tried to leave as frequently as possible; she could not bear the thought of so much life passing her by.

The bar continued to fill up. Newcomers joined their friends in an expanding group along the terrace ledge. It was as if all the young people in Marseille knew one another. Or perhaps it was the familiarity of youth, the way you could become acquainted over a single drink and spend an entire evening chatting.

"Let's skip the restaurant," Alba suggested. "It's fun here."

She'd already pointed out two men with rugged beards; Amina and Lisa joked that they could pick out the most rumpled shirt in any crowd and its owner would be Alba's type.

There wasn't much food on the menu, so they ordered everything—little dishes of olives and spreads, a platter of cured meats. Amina was starving. She'd woken up before dawn with the baby, had barely eaten anything other than the pack of biscuits at the train station. Still, she could see the charm of spending an evening at the bar. Not that she had any interest in the linen-clad men with whom Alba was now exchanging glances. Alba had always been like this: she found someone to flirt with wherever she went. Very quickly, the attention was reciprocated, and then it was up to her to decide how much she wanted from the encounter. Alba's appeal had less to do with her beauty than with her confidence and nonchalance. Lisa and Amina had spent years trying to decipher it, to understand exactly how it worked. There was admiration in their investigation, and of course some envy. Perhaps the envy was related to the fact that Alba's exuberant flirtation had been an aspect of their own youth, before they'd settled into relationships. Amina could not recall whether she'd always thought this; maybe it was only after the birth that age had come into such focus for her.

She remembered a woman telling her, in the last month of her pregnancy, that she should be aware of her diminished desire. This was at a party, and the woman had approached Amina out of the blue to say that after she gave birth to her first child she had not wanted to have sex with her husband for quite a long time. People had a way of opening up to pregnant women, as if they would forgive, or forget, whatever they were told.

"How long?" Amina asked.

"Oh, I can't remember," the woman said. "It was years ago. The point is, no one told me this would happen. That's why I'm telling you now. But don't worry. It will come back. It's your life force."

Amina had taken the woman's words at face value: a simple warning. But afterward, months after the baby was born, she wondered whether the anecdote was intended to have the opposite effect, to draw attention to the woman's restored passion, and mark her sexuality. She hadn't been very young—certainly past her reproductive years, a time when it might seem surprising to talk about desire. Yet she'd seemed fierce, and radiant. She'd seemed, Amina thought in retrospect, to be showing off.

THEY WERE TOO tired to walk along the port as they'd planned and took a taxi back to the flat. They bought a bottle of wine and a pack of cigarettes from a kiosk downstairs, though none of them really smoked anymore.

"Just one glass," Lisa cautioned. "We shouldn't waste all day hungover tomorrow." But they were too sleepy by the time they'd changed out of their clothes. They wandered off to their beds, murmuring good night.

Breakfast was coffee and tartines with jam on a chic plaza. A block away, the streets were lined with fabric shops, elderly men crammed onto benches.

Alba said that she couldn't get a sense of the city, of its age and mood. One minute it seemed ancient, then suddenly youthful.

"It's a harbor," Lisa said. "Port towns are always eclectic." Amina liked the sound of that—the idea of Old World trade, of people stepping ashore, embarking on adventure.

They took a group photo. Alba offered around the pack of cigarettes. They asked the waiter for second cups of coffee.

"This is so great," Amina said. "This may be the best morning I've had in a year."

The waiter turned around and tapped her on the shoulder.

"You can do better," he said in English. "You haven't even tried the pastries."

He took out a lighter from his back pocket and extended the flame to Alba. When he left, Lisa remarked that he sported both a rumpled shirt and a rugged beard.

"Well, then," Alba said, "I guess I have a type."

When he returned with their coffees, he asked if they were sisters. The three of them were wearing flowing black outfits, and they all had brownish hair, though they weren't otherwise very similar.

"Sisters from different mothers," Alba told him. It was unclear whether he understood what this meant.

"Are the sisters on holiday?" He looked boyish despite his dark beard.

"Yes," Alba said. "Do you have any suggestions for us?"

"Have you already taken the ferry?" He named a place Amina couldn't make out. "You must go there. You drink pastis at the docks, and you eat—" He said something else she couldn't catch.

"Great suggestions," Lisa said. "We'll totally do that." It was clear she had no idea what he'd said, either.

A few minutes later, he came back to smoke a cigarette at the empty table next to theirs. It didn't look as if his shift was over, only that he was taking things easy.

"Are you from Marseille?" Alba asked.

He was born in Bordeaux, had moved here a year ago. He felt this was where he really belonged. The city was full of energy, he said. His two good friends from home, with whom he had a band, were also in Marseille.

"You're in a band?" Alba asked.

"We're not Pink Floyd. We just have fun."

"Would love to hear you play," Alba said.

"Would love to play for you," the waiter said.

When he was called back to work, he told them that they were a happy sight: three women having a great morning.

"You're all like sunshine," he said. The awkwardness of the phrase did not diminish its charm.

Afterward, they egged Alba on to ask for his number.

"Can I be bothered?" Alba stretched her arms dramatically. "I mean, I guess it would be fun to have an *amoureux* in Marseille. Handy for holidays."

Amina remembered Alba's way of talking about men—her tone of idleness. It hadn't occurred to her before that *this* might be her allure: the suggestion that she was bored with them even as she was intrigued.

When they got up to leave, Alba told her friends to wait for her. She went inside, where the waiter was standing at the bar. He jotted down something on a piece of paper and handed it to Alba, who walked out smiling.

"I asked him for the name of that place," she explained. "And the thing we're supposed to eat. It's called a *panisse*," she read out from the piece of paper. "And then I invited him for a drink with us."

"How did he react?" Lisa asked.

"Oh," Alba said, "he put on some airs, like he was expecting it. I mean, he isn't as boyish as he looks."

He was seeing a friend that evening, but he could meet up later. Amina and Lisa agreed this was the best arrangement—they'd have a long dinner, then join him for a nightcap.

"Nightcap for me and Lisa," Amina said with a giggle.

"His name is Vincent," Alba added. "Or, should I say, *Van-sun*."

"*Vincent, mon amour*," Lisa cooed.

THERE WERE TWO museums that Amina had suggested visiting when they were making plans in the group chat, though they now decided it would be more fun to be outside. They were feeling so jolly, walking the streets. The encounter with Vincent had cheered them up, given them purpose. It was as if they were all going to meet him for a date that evening. And in a way they were: they'd made their impression as a group, and would do so again, until it was time for Alba to take off with him. This was not so different from their student years, when Amina and Lisa would help Alba in her quests—they must have decided that this was a smoother path than trying to compete with her. Any flirtations of their own happened in private, away from Alba. And perhaps Alba was now a bit old for one-night stands with waiters—after all, she'd readily stated that she wanted a relationship. But this was part of the thrill; a reminder that they were on holiday.

Amina was a little sad to skip the museums—she hadn't been to one in months. Her days were so efficient, and practical. She was feeling the same restlessness she'd experienced on the journey—that there would not be enough time, that she was wasting her trip. It was already past noon; her train back home was the following day.

She didn't tell her friends she'd still like to go to a museum. They would joke that she was an old lady, as they used to when Amina sat alone on a couch at parties, watching people. Was that what it meant to be old—a spectator to interesting things?

Lisa was telling them that they were entering the city's longest-inhabited neighborhood, atop a hill. Winding, narrow streets were lined with pots of flowers. There were many shops, meant to lure tourists with overpriced hats and silk dresses. So many useless, beautiful things: they examined them seriously, one by one. They each bought a hat, scarves, beaded jewelry. When they reached the bottom of the hill, the sea appeared before them, like a celebration. Alba said that they might as well take the ferry, as Vincent had suggested.

"I thought that was just an excuse to get his number," Lisa said. "We have reservations for lunch."

"It'll give us something to talk about when we meet him," Alba said. "And it's a tip from a local."

"I agree," Amina said. "We might not get to see anything like this."

They had some trouble finding the correct ferry. Most people were boarding another one, to go swimming at the *calanques*. Theirs turned out to be a small motorboat that would take them across the bay. The young boy checking tickets advised them to sit in the front, so they wouldn't get wet.

Soon enough, they were in open sea, pushing forth against crashing waves. Even where the boy had suggested, they were sprayed by water. Lisa and Alba cheered with every thrust and descent of the boat. Amina tried to appear calm, though she was at that moment imagining a disaster, and its aftermath. She pictured her husband telling the baby that Mama wasn't coming back, and the miscomprehension on the baby's face. She had tears in her eyes from the scenario; she was annoyed with Vincent for suggesting such a trip.

The village, when they finally arrived, was utterly unspectacular. There was a single café, where they stepped off the boat. Farther down the boardwalk, food trucks were indeed selling *panisse*, which looked something like fried dough.

They walked a little way inland, though there was no center to speak of. A bunch of teenagers were smoking on a bench, loud, unpleasant music thumping from somewhere in their midst.

"Let's just go back to the café," Lisa suggested. "We can have lunch there and take the next boat to the city."

There were only chips, which they bought with their pastis. They asked the waiter how much water they should add to dilute the fragrant, milky liquid he'd poured. He was a young boy; at first glance, he looked just like the one who'd taken their tickets on the boat. Perhaps the two of them were brothers.

"Depends how drunk you want to get," the boy replied. He offered them second rounds on the house as their boat was approaching.

"We have to leave soon," Amina said. "But thanks."

"Let's dunk them," Alba said.

"She knows what she's talking about," the boy said.

Maybe he wasn't a mere boy. Maybe they were a little tipsy. In any case, the ride back to the city did not feel so bumpy.

On board, a young woman asked Amina to take her photo. She posed seductively, pouting her lips without any hint of self-consciousness. Then she took the phone back and examined the pictures.

"Thank you *sooo* much," she said. "I'm traveling alone, so I always have to ask."

"How do you like Marseille?" Amina asked.

"Oh, it's so fun. And this little village was amazing."

"What did you like about it?" Alba asked, only slightly condescending.

"Cézanne's house, of course," the woman said. "I imagined him painting there, seeing the view from up top."

The friends exchanged glances. Was that why Vincent had told them to go to the village? How had they failed to realize its significance?

"Where else have you been?" Lisa asked.

That morning, the young woman had visited the two museums they'd skipped. She had tickets to see a dance show later. She was taking a train early the next day to Spain, where she would meet up with her boyfriend to walk the path of St. James. She was not religious, she clarified, but she would consider herself *spiritual*. She had recently graduated from university and was taking a year off to travel.

Amina was startled by just how much they had learned about the young woman within minutes. She was still young enough that she could sum up her life in a continuous narrative; she hadn't asked them any questions, perhaps believing that her year of travels was something extraordinary. Amina didn't tell her that she and her friends had all done something similar after graduation.

It didn't seem very interesting now. In fact, Amina felt a little tired on the young woman's behalf—all those trains she had to take, the cheap hostels, the plazas of every city which blurred into one another. Lisa and Alba had stopped listening and were deep in a conversation of their own.

"Wow," Alba said when they stepped off the boat. "You had a lot of patience for her."

"She was just young," Amina said, feeling generous now that the conversation was over.

They discussed what to do before dinner. They could go back to the flat to change, though it was in the opposite direction from the restaurant. They were all disheveled from the wind, sprayed with seawater.

"It's Alba's call," Lisa said. "She's the one meeting her *amoureux*."

"Oh, I'll just put on some lipstick," Alba said. "I don't want to drag everyone back for my sake. Vincent can take it or leave it."

In the end, they sat on a bench by the harbor, idly watching the crowds. Amina called her husband to check if everything was all right.

"We've had a great day," her husband said. "*Someone* was on her best behavior. Don't worry about us."

She was grateful to him for saying that, and a bit envious that she'd missed out. And now it was nearly the baby's bedtime. Afterward, her husband would pour himself a glass of wine and watch something before going to read in bed. Whereas she still had so many hours ahead of her.

THERE WAS A mix-up with their reservation: they were given seats at the bar until one of the tables cleared. Lisa kept repeating that she wasn't pleased about this, but the waiter did not take her very seriously.

They were tired, and hungry. The barstools weren't comfortable. Half-heartedly, they discussed plans for the next day: perhaps they could make it to one of the museums before Amina's train.

"That all depends on Alba's night out," Lisa said, trying to lift their group spirit. "You should text him now."

"I'll wait a bit," Alba said. "He's probably out with his friend." Amina couldn't tell whether it was for their sake that Alba was demonstrating nonchalance. Still, Alba wrote a message a few minutes later, telling Vincent to meet them at the restaurant.

The job was done. And their food had arrived. They were all in a better mood. They discussed ideas for another, longer trip, a few months later.

"How about that music festival in Barcelona?" Alba suggested. "Get Amina back on track."

"I just need to figure out logistics," Amina said, "but it should be doable."

"It's good to see you liven up," Alba went on. "When you arrived yesterday, I thought . . . she's had a tough year."

"Really?" Amina said. "I was feeling totally fine."

"It's more the overall change."

"And?" Amina said. "What'd you notice?"

"Darling, you're always fabulous. You just need some sleep. And maybe a haircut."

Amina felt a shudder of annoyance at the bluntness of the comment, and also at its blindness—that signs of her transformation should be guessed at from her appearance. She held back from saying something bitter. She shouldn't make a big deal of it, she thought. This was the way they'd always been with one another. But it was true that she felt, at that moment, defeated.

There was no response from Vincent when they finished eating, so they each ordered another glass of wine and asked the waiter for the dessert menu. In the end, they'd never been given a table, and now the waiter was telling them that the seats at the bar were also reserved.

"You still have some time," he offered. "Just wanted to let you know."

"It's okay," Lisa said curtly. "We'll have dessert somewhere else."

After they paid, they walked toward the harbor, which was now utterly different than when they had stepped off the boat. The boardwalk was teeming with people trying to get into bars. Girls in high heels, shaky on their legs; boys dressed comically like businessmen, in blazers and dress shoes.

"Where did all these people come from?" Alba asked.

The air smelled of perfume and hair gel.

"Let's get out of here," Lisa said, leading them toward a side street, and up to the shopping avenue they'd walked the previous evening. The stores were closed, the pavements, empty. The booming sound of music from the harbor reached them as if through a membrane. They took another turn, into a lifeless, dirty neighborhood, though none of them wanted to suggest they should just go home. Alba's phone buzzed.

"Finally," Lisa said. "Someone's playing hard to get."

Alba was silent for a moment. Her face fell, just a little. Then she read out the message.

It would have been lovely to join them, Vincent wrote, but he was already back home. He hadn't met up with his friend, after all. If they were around the following afternoon, he'd be playing music at a café, some distance from the center. He could send them details.

"Well," Alba said. "I guess I wrote too late."

"Do you want to go tomorrow?" Amina asked. "We could make it if it's early enough."

"Can't be bothered," Alba said. "And I can't believe he's arrogant enough to suggest we come to watch him tuning his guitar on our holiday."

"It's your call," Amina said, though the whole thing now sounded a bit pathetic.

They turned around and headed in the direction of the flat.

"You know," Alba said, "the city's grown on me. I didn't know what to make of it at first. It's so vibrant. And I find it amazing that most people we met today were our age, at most."

"Sorry to break it to you," Amina said. "But they were all younger by, like, a decade."

And perhaps this had dawned on all of them, like an answer, though they hadn't realized until then that there'd been a question. It had never been a question, not yet. It *was* still their turn.

"Oh my god." Lisa said. "What if . . . what if he thought we were just a bunch of aunties?"

"Don't be ridiculous," Alba said. "I already thought about it—he's at most five, maybe six years younger. Besides, we don't show our age."

"I was kidding," Lisa said. "Obviously we're not *aunties.*"

Still, they were startled by Alba's response. That she'd even considered the question, and addressed it, rather than laugh it off as she always did. That she'd made a decision for all of them.

Amina tried to recall their exchange at the café, the way Vincent had flattered them. It hadn't occurred to her that he might be doing so out of vanity, to make anyone who crossed his path adore him.

They'd reached their building.

"We're definitely having a nightcap," Lisa said. Alba offered to go to the kiosk to get a bottle of wine. Really, they were all tired, though they wouldn't let on, for the sake of their last evening.

Then they remembered that the bottle they'd bought the previous night was unopened, and climbed slowly up the stairs.

Ghosts

Last night she came to me again. We were in the room, facing each other on opposite beds, our legs not reaching the marble floor. We hadn't aged at all. Once again, Damla's hair was long. The thick braid hung down her shoulder. I'd never seen anything so beautiful. We were wearing the matching yellow shorts my mother had bought the day before Damla arrived.

In the dream, her eyes were no different than those staring from televisions and magazines. But this time, she'd come back to tell me something.

SHE CAME BEFORE summer unfurled, before the boats came down from the shipyard, under skies of drifting clouds.

There was no ceremony, no change from the way things had always been. There was work for her in the restaurant kitchen. A bed from our grandmother's house was moved to my room. My mother bought us the matching shorts.

I took her to the black rock on the shore, showed her how to search with her hand for the crack underneath, in the water. She picked up a shell from the water, took it to her ear, and listened. How had she known about the shells, up in the hills in that dark house?

WE BROUGHT HER back from the house in the hills.

There were other children there, huddled around Damla, watching us. We sat opposite them in the dark room.

"Do you ever hear from him?" Damla's mother asked. She wasn't too proud to plead.

I was told I shouldn't say a word about Uncle, pretend he'd disappeared and not mention that he came by from time to time. But I knew that Uncle always came back when he needed something. He'd even gone with Captain on a tour for a week, as a cook. That was Captain's favor to my father. Because Uncle was good for nothing.

"We'll take her," my father said, nodding his head at Damla. She didn't look up. There was bitter tea, and a bowl of sweets in wrappers. "We'll bring her back at the end of summer."

"The girls will sleep in one room," he said. "They're basically sisters."

HER HANDS WERE like water, like sand.

She cut branches of pepper and draped them over lampshades. She brought stones to line the windowsills.

"What's all this?" my mother asked, but I saw that she was taking in the sight.

She showed me how to make a kite. The tail was long and ruffled, red and green. We took the kite to the hill and set it free. It turned around once, then came back to our feet like a dog.

Dogs followed her, too, and she spoke to them with her fingers, finding the knuckle behind their ears, the soft, folding skin of their foreheads. Soon there were two that followed us like the kite's tail. She held out her hand to them when we came back to the village. The dogs understood they would have to wait, and they listened to her command.

THESE DAYS IT wouldn't be allowed, but back then there was no fuss. We may even have thought we were helping them, up in that dark house in the hills. We were always paying Uncle's debts.

She came with us in the truck. Her mother came out of the house, carrying a bag. One of the children, a little boy, cried.

When my father started the truck, they all went inside. I saw her mother looking from the window as we drove away, looking so intently I thought we would swerve.

"That woman," my grandmother used to say. "Who knows what she'll do."

We were always paying Uncle's debts. And we were always covering them up, blaming them on others.

COMING DOWN TO our village from the hills, you first saw the almond trees, then the crowd of roosters. The coffeehouse patched with oleander, Captain's house behind the crooked pine, our restaurant painted blue and white.

Then the sea like a crack, like the world opening up.

"You're probably used to this," visitors would tell us. "It's all the same to you."

THE BOATS ARRIVED on wheels, rolling down the main street, down the sand, into water. Blue and green and red, swaying their barren masts, like the sea dressing up for a wedding.

I showed her *Penelope*. That winter, the boat had been painted green. Its name spread red along the prow.

In the mornings we would go down to the cabin, to sit among planks of wood. That summer, before the tours started, Captain and two boys from the village were putting in new cabinets. If they saw us, they'd give us something. A bottle of Coca-Cola, things left behind by foreign children. A beaded bracelet, a plastic ball. A T-shirt that read *Amsterdam*.

"Girls, girls, girls," Captain said one time, when he found us sitting inside a cabinet. "What're you doing here again, with all the ghosts?"

When Captain left, Damla asked me, "Do you think it's true?"

I didn't know.

"We'll wait here and see if they come," she said.

Before *Penelope* left the bay, we waited in the cabin each day, to see if Captain was right.

I HEARD THERE is a poster of her in the coffeehouse. No doubt she must be staring with that haunted look that won her fame.

I went to see the film by myself. And then I went again. I would have said she was no different, except her hair.

I heard that the villagers boast she's like family to them. I couldn't say, about family. I haven't been back in years.

BEFORE SHE CAME, I watched her invisible shadow growing by my side.

"The girl must be getting older."

"The girl must be in school now."

One time when Uncle came, they said, "What will we do about the girl?"

"Girl" meant half kin.

Uncle didn't respond. He didn't worry about such things, about all the trouble he'd caused. He would appear out of the blue, smelling dusty. My mother and grandmother would cook a feast, even though he never smiled. He put up his feet in the living room, spent hours snoring on the divan. He walked up and down the main street, waiting for the coffeehouse to fill up. He played cards with Captain's brothers. Then he was gone.

After Damla arrived, my mother pulled me aside in the garden.

"Does she tell you anything?" she asked. "Does she talk about her mother?"

I shook my head.

"Does she talk about your uncle?"

"No."

"Don't believe her, anyway," my mother said.

WHEN VISITORS ON *Penelope* anchored for a night by the village, we set up the long table on the beach, away from the road, even if it was sandy there, and dark. At night the waves washed up to their ankles. That's what the visitors enjoyed. A taste of life in the waves. Captain always brought his tours to us—ten, twelve, fifteen people, ordering bottle after bottle, and all the dishes to taste.

If I went outside with the appetizer tray, someone would ask, "Does the little girl always work? Doesn't she go to school?"

"Of course she does." My father laughed, "But we just can't keep her out of here. She'll grow up to be a chef."

"What do you want to be?" the visitors asked, and before I could respond, they said, "You can be a doctor. You can be a teacher."

I mostly stayed in the kitchen helping with the dishes, not ladling too much on the plates, as I'd been told. That summer, Damla cleaned the fish.

"The girl can gut," my father said. You'd think she was a sea person.

Some visitors thought we were twins. But visitors were always a little blind. They thought the almond trees were plums. They ordered sea bass we bought in the city, and they said how good it was to eat the fish of these seas. They inhaled the smell of charred skin as if it would heal them.

They offered us bits of food they bought along the main street—almonds, bread, cucumbers. They were always eating, the visitors. Out of politeness we accepted all the things they offered us from our own village.

•

BEFORE DAMLA CAME, my grandmother would tell me stories at night.

Once there was a woman who made her children disappear. She lived far away in the mountains, and her face was like dust. Her children grew paler each day, until you couldn't see them. The woman looked right through her own children.

I was so scared, I couldn't ask if the woman was still there, in the mountains. My grandmother said that those nameless things whirled around her. They never left her alone.

I TOOK DAMLA up on the hill, past the house where Melike used to live, and down to the cove behind the pines. She walked into the water, up to her ankles. I said she had to make herself very soft, very light, and she crouched in the shallow water, her shirt billowing behind her. Then she got up and walked deeper, and I saw her arms and hair spread out on the water. And before the moment she thrashed madly, I saw her float.

HAD THE SEA always been blue and black? Had clouds always smiled or frowned? So they did when she arrived. The village crisped, like almond trees blushing, like the sea at high tide, the rocks carved purple along the shore. So, when she arrived, our village was beautiful.

SHE LOVED CAPTAIN, too, and I didn't mind. We watched him climb the mast with his red bandanna. We sat with him when he mended the sails.

He played us music without words. "This music will take you out of here, girls," he said.

There was no one like Captain.

He taught us knots—simple, sturdy, sturdiest—and we repeated with our fumbling hands. We practiced down in the cabin, lines stretched between us.

IT'S A DIFFERENT place, where Captain lives now, with uniformed staff and pleasant smells. I once went myself. A polite, meek man rolled him out in his wheelchair. He wasn't much older than Captain, but standing on his own two legs. That's what embarrassed me. I told the man he could take the afternoon off.

I'd brought chocolates with me, and a painting of the sea.

He wasn't what he used to be, our Captain.

I heard that she arranges for all of it, the room and the man who wheels him around.

"God bless her," Captain said to me that day. "Taking care of a near stranger."

THAT SUMMER, WE hollowed out time.

Down in the cove, there was a world within the seaweed and pine, with valleys of cones and pebbles.

There was the top of the hill, where we stood watching the village curled like a shell, green and dusty.

There was the cabinet, where we fit our hushed bodies, waiting for ghosts.

There was our grandmother's porch at night, on the wood divan, beneath the mosquito net softly sighing, cicadas lighting up the village with their sound.

At night we lay on our backs in the dark, listening to the ceiling fan, scared of nothing.

"Who is Melike?" she asked one time. I didn't ask her how she'd learned that name. I understood that there were things she already knew.

I didn't know too much more than the name, the way it hovered above the village.

"She used to live there," I said, pointing toward the hills. "She was mad."

"What happened to her?"

"She died, but she didn't leave."

"Did you ever see her, afterward?"

"No."

They said she mostly visited girls before their weddings, to warn them.

"About what?"

I shrugged. Which was different than a lie. I barely remembered the wedding myself, Melike in the white dress and red ribbons. Uncle without a smile.

I patched things together vaguely, like getting up for water at night.

A COUPLE OF boys had gone to the graveyard one night and summoned ghosts. They came to the kitchen door to tell us, trying to impress Damla, until my father shooed them away.

"Don't be so friendly with boys," he told Damla.

"What did you hear?" Damla asked the boys.

" 'I'm a ghost! I live in the graveyard!' "

"I don't believe it," Damla said.

That night, when we were back in our room, she told me, "We're going to call Melike."

"What if the other ones come?" I said. "The ones that never leave you alone."

"That's good, too."

WHAT DID WE know, two girls, irrelevant as ghosts?

•

DAMLA DIDN'T COME back the following summer. And anyway, business was bad at the restaurant, without the customers Captain brought. That's what we always called him, even if it might have seemed to visitors that we were humoring an invalid.

My father and I went to the house on the hills to bring Damla back to the village, and I said nothing to stop him.

Her hair was short, the way everyone would know her in her fame. She watched me silently across the room, undoing all that we'd seen.

Two girls, irrelevant to all the world. It had never occurred to us that we were anything but spectators, that we could disturb the world with our touch.

"Leave us alone," her mother said. "She doesn't want to come with you."

FOR MELIKE TO talk to us, Damla said, we would have to make it possible for her to speak to us. We sat down in the cabin, our fingers pressed on a shell.

"Melike," Damla said. "We want to talk to you."

"Melike, do you have something to tell us?"

The boat rocked gently. We heard the swishing of pebbles. The shell began to slide.

But Captain came to the cabin and told us we had to leave. They were taking off for the week.

"You don't want to be trapped in here, do you?"

Every night, waiting for the boat's return, we talked about the shell, which had begun to tell us something. Together, we were fearless. We owned the world with our stories.

I told Damla that Uncle had been married another time—after he'd disappeared from their house on the hills. That's all I knew.

"But he was already married," Damla said.

"Yes."

"That's why she came back, to tell us about it."

WHEN THE BOAT returned from its trip, unloading the roasted tourists back on land, we tore up letters and scattered them around the cabin floor. We pushed the portholes open. We piled cards and backgammon pieces on the floor. We brought branches, pine cones, more shells. But nothing stirred.

Perhaps we could try with the sails. We imagined them opening and flapping in conversation. We thought we should untie the ropes and set them free.

AND THEN THE evenings were colder, pebbles combed the shore louder at high tide. We had special names for each other, a secret pact. Damla said she would be back the next summer, and we would learn to sail. And later, she told me, we'd live on a boat, the two of us. We'd see the world.

WE WERE WALKING to the boat when we saw Uncle. He was standing with Captain, laughing.

I saw Damla shrink.

"That girl, skulking about," adults used to say. I saw, then, what they saw.

When we came closer and stood by Captain's side, Uncle looked first at me, then at her.

"Tell your mother I'll be home for dinner tonight," he told me.

We went to the cove instead and sat among the pine cones.

"Are they friends, then?" Damla asked. "Him and Captain?"

I shrugged.

"Does he ever ask about me?"

I picked up a cone and threw it in the water.

"Yes," I said. "Sometimes."

"Why would Captain want to be his friend?"

I shrugged again.

The next day, when Captain was sleeping in the cabin, we untied the sturdiest knots on deck, impatient now for a sign, for the ghost to come.

•

AT THE END of the summer, the bed was carried back. The yellow-checkered shorts folded and put away.

Much later, when we saw her on the television, my mother would say she'd been right all along.

"Thankless girl," she said. "After all we did for her."

•

NOTHING WAS SAID when Captain fell off the mast.

We watched him from the cabin steps, climbing up, though he didn't see us.

We might have stepped forward to warn him about the ropes. We were thinking of the words, but waiting at the same time for Melike to appear. One more moment, and we'd rush to say something.

What could we have done, two girls like ghosts?

High up, with his red bandanna, we watched Captain falter. He swayed, reached out with one arm to hold on.

We stood watching for some time, after the rope gave way, speeding Captain to the ground. First there was the noise, and then he lay still.

And there was a moment, just before he came crashing, that he floated in the air.

The Guest

Nehla and I had been together for almost a year when she told me she would be traveling to her hometown for her sister's wedding. At that point I knew very little about her family, but whenever she talked about them, it was with a different tone, a pure and immense love.

She was going to be away for almost a month. There would be preparations before the wedding; she wanted to help her sister and mother, who were already overwhelmed. But even as she told me about the plans, she didn't invite me to join her. When I finally said that I hated the idea of being apart for so long, she told me matter-of-factly that it would be inappropriate for her to bring a partner to her hometown without having a serious attachment. There was no apology in her tone, at least not on behalf of her family, though she said it with sympathy toward me, as if she were asking me to understand the delicacy of the situation.

"Let's get engaged, then," I said. I had been thinking about it for several months by that point. I'd known soon into our relationship that I'd met a woman of incredible strength and beauty; that I shouldn't test my great fortune by waiting too long. Nehla let out a laugh, bright and childish, then came over to give me a hug. We went out to dinner, ordered a bottle of wine to celebrate.

That Sunday, her phone conversation with her parents was longer than usual. She had stayed over at my place the previous night, and in the morning we prepared a lavish breakfast, still in the mood for celebration. I made excuses to go into the living room while she talked, to get a sense of the mood. Nehla's voice sounded more solemn than joyful, although I couldn't understand the words. Afterward, she told me that her family were very happy, even if her sister had joked that Nehla was stealing the attention from her own wedding. Nehla smiled as she told me this, though she looked troubled. I asked her if anything else was the matter, and she assured me that there was nothing at all, just a lot of preparations ahead that preoccupied her.

I JOINED NEHLA two weeks after she left. It was a long journey—across the ocean, then two flights to the hometown, after which I walked the short distance from the tarmac to the terminal. Nehla and her parents were waiting for me behind the glass. They wore expressions of utter seriousness, as if my arrival were a tragedy. During the drive to town, I asked Nehla to translate some things—how glad I was to be there, how much I looked forward to the wedding—but I was too fatigued to say anything more meaningful.

I was to stay at the home of Nehla's uncle, who lived in the same building as the parents. I'd been told about the arrangement only some days before my trip, and was annoyed that I was being treated like a teenage boy, rather than Nehla's fiancé. Still, the uncle and his wife greeted me with much ceremony, scurrying about before I went to bed, bringing me all manner of things that I might need. They'd asked Nehla to tell me that I should feel entirely at home, should go to the fridge to help myself—after all, the aunt said, it was stocked with dishes prepared for my arrival.

In the following days, the uncle and Nehla's father took me around town. We went to the river, the new mall, the clock tower, and the farm of a cousin. Every trip was bracketed with extravagant meals at traditional and modern restaurants, as well as the homes of various relatives. Even breakfast was an event, with tables filled to spilling. I'd never tasted so many delicacies in such a short time. It was as if, not being able to speak to me, the family had decided instead to supply me with a constant flow of food.

I was taken aback by the informal segregation on these occasions—the men eating while the women hurried to bring out more food, refill plates, clear up. Afterward the women gathered in the kitchen, chatting among themselves. Nehla would be there, too, and I wished she would come out to keep me company instead. Once or twice I wandered to the kitchen to talk to her, and she welcomed me with a smile, though I felt out of place and returned to my seat among the uncles, cousins, and my soon-to-be brother-in-law. He was a sulking man, and I had not warmed to him. Some months back, Nehla had shared with me her worries that her sister was making a mistake. She'd tried talking to her about it without success, and felt that it was not her place to insist any further. Besides, she said, her sister must think the same about Nehla's life.

ONE AFTERNOON I accompanied Nehla to a jewelry shop to pick up the wedding rings, as well as a bracelet the parents had had made for Nehla's sister. I was beyond myself with excitement for this time alone, and suggested getting a coffee after we completed our errands. Nehla took me to a patisserie that had been a staple of her life during her high school years. It was here, she told me, that she and her friends gathered to eat sour cherry cake and drink Coca-Cola after school; it was these same forged iron tables that had witnessed the first heartaches of Nehla's life.

I joked that it was a bit difficult for me to imagine any love affairs in this town, with the constant policing of the relatives. I'd meant the comment lightly, though I suppose I let my frustration seep through.

"I know," Nehla said, "so much of our lives were lived in secret. You must find all of this totally backward." Once again, there was kindness in her tone, without any hint of self-consciousness or apology.

We each ordered a slice of the sour cherry cake, and Nehla told me with girlish enthusiasm about the friends of her youth. The patisserie tables were occupied by other couples, a pair of elderly women, and a group of teenagers erupting in hysterical laughter, perhaps like Nehla and her friends years ago. It was a soulful, welcoming place, with its old-fashioned cakes and pastel colors, weathered with time but nonetheless alive. I asked Nehla whether she was still in touch with any of her school friends. Sadly, she said, they had grown apart. It would be no use contacting them now, because their lives were so different. And yet it wouldn't surprise her to learn that these friends were still very close with one another. This for her was the most lamentable aspect of leaving a community, a real one that had grown alongside you from the day you were born, whose members had once been unquestionably close to you, without fuss or ceremony, without even having to exert effort. I wanted to take her in my arms and comfort her. I was, also, shamefully pleased by her rupture with the past, as if this meant that

I would have her to myself, that there was less about her I could not relate to.

On our way back we circumvented the main road, which was blocked by a convoy of campaign buses. Loudspeakers blasted a repetitive song. Nehla told me that it was a playful rephrasing of an older political tune known to most. Elections were coming up, and every street was covered with flags and posters without order, though there was little doubt that the ruling party would emerge victorious once again, despite all accusations of corruption and human rights violations, as well as the total ravaging of the country's natural resources. Since our first date, Nehla and I had discussed the situation. We'd even attended a demonstration together to protest the imprisonment of a journalist held without trial. As we were entering her parents' neighborhood, Nehla said it was a good thing the elections were still some time away—they would not taint the wedding celebrations.

That was one good thing, I agreed. It unfortunately looked as if the results would deflate everyone's spirits.

"That's not what I meant," Nehla said. "I'm just glad I won't have to get into too many arguments with my family." She added, "Most of them support the government, you know."

I was startled. I couldn't understand why she had kept this information from me, and told her as much.

"I thought you knew," Nehla said. "I mean, so much of the country supports them."

But she was on such good terms with her family, I protested. She seemed so fond of everyone. It was unbelievable that these people would have such untenable values. Nehla looked at me quizzically. For a moment I thought she'd contradict me, or say that I couldn't possibly grasp the complexity of the situation, but instead she shrugged. We had reached the apartment, and with a forlorn look on her face, she rang the doorbell.

SOME DAYS BEFORE the wedding, a dinner was thrown in our honor, to celebrate our engagement. Nehla explained to me that her parents had decided on it at the last minute; it would make them feel better, she said, to be part of the whole affair. She and I already lived so far away that she didn't want to deny her parents this pleasure. I was already exhausted by all the gatherings, yanked from one to the next with no concern for my preferences. Still, I felt I had no choice in the matter.

Seated next to me at the dinner was a man named Suad who had studied abroad. I guessed that he was a cousin, although I didn't have a good understanding of how everyone was related. People whose genealogy were so removed as to be impossible to explain were considered brothers and sisters; run-ins with neighbors could not be rushed because they were like family; one afternoon, when the superintendent carried up some heavy boxes, he was invited inside for lunch. We'd planned on going out, but Nehla asked whether I would mind staying to eat with him—he was as dear to her as an uncle.

The cousin, Suad, had completed a one-year degree in business administration and was now managing the family trade, importing glass objects. He was resentful toward capitalism—*ironically*, I thought, *for a businessman*—and "the West," with its corrupting forces. This was what he talked about for the majority of the dinner, demanding my attention. I vaguely agreed with his arguments, nodding my head as he presented claim upon claim about the imperialist scheme to crumble his nation.

"Look at the state of us," he said. "And meanwhile the West continues to prosper."

Did he think, I asked, that his government held any responsibility for the state of affairs?

"What do you mean?" Suad asked.

Or, I continued, trying to sound humorous, did Suad think that the government was indeed put in place by these corrupting forces, to hold the country back?

Suad roared with laughter. Then he shouted something across the table at Nehla's father, who smiled briefly and turned back to his own conversation. I glanced at Nehla, seated next to her father, and I could tell that she was upset.

After dinner, Nehla's uncle made a speech and put on our engagement rings—thin gold bands we'd picked out that morning in the presence of Nehla's parents, who'd insisted on paying for them. I hadn't been allowed to pay for anything since my arrival, which was starting to weigh on me; I didn't know how I could return the family's hospitality, and I did not like to feel indebted.

The uncle kissed us both on our cheeks, then moved aside for everyone else to do the same. Afterward I followed Nehla to the kitchen, where tea and coffee were being prepared, and asked if everything was all right. She shrugged. This wasn't the time to bring it up, she said, but she wished that I wouldn't get into meaningless arguments.

"I wasn't getting into an argument," I told her. "I was taken hostage by your cousin and his conspiracy theories."

"He's not my cousin," Nehla said. "We only invited him to keep you company."

MY FLIGHT BACK was the morning after the wedding. Nehla would return a week later. I'd booked my ticket with a daylong layover, so I could be back in the city where I'd spent much of my university summers, traveling, working odd jobs, doing internships. I'd wanted Nehla to come with me, so I could take her around the narrow streets and scenic plazas of the city, which she'd never visited.

It had been a tense parting. On my last days I'd made little effort to seem enthusiastic about the various trips and meals proposed to me, and had finally been left to my own devices while everyone else was busy with preparations.

The wedding itself struck me as something garish. The bride and groom were swarmed by guests, not speaking a word to each other, not enjoying the occasion in the least. It bothered me to think that my wedding to Nehla might look just like this, a mad enactment of a ritual that brought no joy to the couple being celebrated. What bothered me more, though, was the fact that I could not share these thoughts with Nehla; she would shut me down, would tell me I was being judgmental or narrow-minded.

I TOOK A taxi to my hotel and spent some hours enjoying my solitude and anonymity. There were no messages from Nehla, and I didn't text her. I took a shower and dressed. Nehla's aunt had insisted on washing my laundry before I left, and had returned everything crisply ironed. *I should buy a present for her*, I thought, *and post it from the airport the next day.*

Outside was a bright, warm evening. I was struck by the style and polish of the city people, perhaps even more so after Nehla's hometown. Once again, I wished that Nehla were with me, that I could take her around the city. At the same time I was aware that I wished for the person she'd been to me before our trip.

Whether she had actually changed, or unraveled in some way, I didn't know. Still, I could not picture that other Nehla—among her relatives, tending solemnly to kitchen preparations—in this setting.

I wandered around the historic district, taking turns haphazardly, remembering the person I had been two decades prior: naive, romantic, unpractical. I came upon a bookshop where I'd spent many hours attending events and chatting with the staff. It looked exactly the same, with its brightly painted exterior, the clutter of old shelves and tables inside spilling over with books, the back wall covered with Post-it notes from visitors. There was an event that evening, open to the public. It was a panel discussion by three writers, whose recent books were tangentially connected by the topic of immigration. I thought it a strange grouping; the topic seemed forced, as if simply to appeal to contemporary issues. Still, I had nothing better to do.

A crowd had already gathered outside. There were drinks and appetizers on a table. I poured myself a glass of wine. I hadn't eaten all day and was content to pick at the olives and crisps, relieved I wouldn't be subjected to yet another dinner with family members I didn't know.

Suddenly I felt a tap on my shoulder. Behind me, a woman with bright lipstick and smooth chestnut hair stood beaming.

"Karolina," I exclaimed, and opened my arms in an embrace. We'd been colleagues years ago, working at the same nonprofit organization. I recalled, from the bits and pieces I'd seen on social media, that Karolina was now the director of the organization, and had settled in the city, where its headquarters were located. She didn't seem very surprised to see me. After all, visitors were constantly passing through the city, for its charm and central location. She introduced me to some people before saying that she'd go inside to greet the speakers; she was tasked with introducing them for the event.

My new acquaintances felt instantly familiar; we'd all worked in similar fields, even knew people in common. When I mentioned my recent trip to Nehla's hometown, they offered their views about the probable, and disastrous, outcome of the elections, one that would have serious consequences for the region and beyond.

When the speakers appeared, we took our seats in the front row and agreed to continue the conversation afterward. Karolina fiddled with the microphone for a moment with exaggerated concentration before welcoming us. She made an eloquent introduction, raising some of the questions that all three of the books dealt with. Her manner was at once casual and serious, and her presence magnetic—even more so than her charisma in person, perhaps because of the way she controlled her voice, speaking in a deep and sensual tone. I suddenly recalled that something had happened between us, years ago, following a fundraiser. It wasn't anything serious; I wondered whether Karolina even recalled the event—I couldn't be certain that I was remembering correctly myself. Still, I could see now why I'd been attracted to her. I thought fleetingly about Nehla and her parents, what they must be up to at that very moment. They seemed worlds away. I felt a pang—of loss, perhaps, or impossibility—imagining just how out of place they would be in such a setting.

Karolina had stepped offstage; I nodded at her, discreetly giving her the thumbs up. She nodded back and smiled.

One of the speakers was talking about definitions of community. Our current use of the term, he said, could denote something as superficial as an aesthetic demarcation, a group of people who shared a curated lifestyle.

"A warm and fuzzy term," he said, "that is little more than a consumerist fantasy." But what if, he continued, we were to broaden our definition beyond our own curated image; what if we allowed our communities to become imperfect, even ungainly? We'd grown so accustomed to discarding everything in our lives that needed repair, he said. This was true of our material belongings as well as our social and cultural ones: we could abandon them without a second thought, without any consideration of the waste, the wearing down of social fabric.

At this point, there was some commotion in the back. I turned around to see that a man had wandered to the table of drinks and snacks. He was visibly drunk and was pouring the remnants of various bottles into a plastic cup. He had placed his bags and what appeared to be a heap of clothing on an empty seat.

Karolina got up and, crouching to be inconspicuous, went over to the table. I turned my attention back to the discussion, though I was aware of the low hum coming from the back, Karolina's voice and the man's.

The next speaker offered a more spiritual perspective. She mentioned various religious traditions that treated newcomers to a community as guests of God. Even in fairy tales, she went on, those who accepted beggars into their homes were always rewarded. These must have been the ideas she'd prepared to present, but it was now clear that she should say something else, in relation to the scene happening behind us.

Karolina had escorted the man away from the table and was whispering something to him.

"I've always loved this bookshop," the speaker continued, "because it is a place of gathering, because it has always received strangers with open arms." She stopped short of making the point too obvious; after all, Karolina was trying to get rid of the man. I glanced back at her and saw that she'd gone back to the table and was hurriedly placing snacks on a napkin while the man stood some feet away, drinking out of the plastic cup. Then, suddenly, he began to cry. It was a sound like a moan, a deranged, drawn-out wail. At this point, one of the bookshop staff came out and, nodding to Karolina that he would take care of it, held the man by the arm and walked away with him.

The first speaker had reclaimed the microphone and set the conversation back on track.

AFTER THE TALK, I found Karolina and the others by the table. I'd gone inside to buy all three books, somewhat out of obligation. Perhaps Nehla would be interested in the book about the role of the stranger in fairy tales and religions. This was one of the things that had puzzled and intrigued me about Nehla when we first met: the way she held tight to enchantment, refused to see the world as purely rational.

There were more bottles of wine on the table, and fresh plates of food. We congratulated Karolina on her introduction and said that the event had been a success.

"That scene was really uncomfortable," Karolina said, reaching for a cracker. "The man wanted me to pack some food for him. And then he just started crying like that, out of the blue."

"You handled it perfectly," someone said.

"Poor man," Karolina said, "I mean, he was completely wasted."

WALKING TO DINNER—two of the speakers had joined us, and Karolina was leading the way to a restaurant she said we'd all love—I saw that I had missed a call from Nehla. I put the phone back in my pocket. It would be inconvenient to talk to her just then. I would have to keep the others waiting or tell them to order without me. I couldn't simply tell Nehla that I'd run into some people and was now on my way to dinner. I would need to explain the who and the how. And I guessed that Nehla would want to talk as well, perhaps about my visit, what people had thought of me. I could feel myself tensing up, preparing my arguments. I realized that I'd begun going over the events of my visit, combing through them for all the instances for which I could be found at fault. I didn't feel up to a fight, if that was what would emerge. I decided I would call her later, even though, by the time we were done with dinner, it would probably be too late.

Practicality

After it was over—the sorting and cleaning, the signing of papers—and my brother and sisters had returned to their homes, I spent a week in my mother's house. It was mostly empty, save for a bed, the kitchen table, and the wicker chair where my mother used to sit for long hours, looking out at the garden.

In the last years, that sight had saddened me. Seeing my mother immobile, her gaze fixed outside, I would suggest taking her to the garden, or try and distract her with a story, desperate for some assurance, for a sign of my mother's life force.

My siblings had started to talk openly about the steps we must take. I was grateful for their competence, even as I was angered by their bluntness. The only time I reproached my older brother, he asked me somewhat impatiently whether it would be better to ignore the matter completely. In the end, we had found a young woman to live with our mother.

On the morning of our mother's passing, the young woman phoned me first with the news. Even in my shock, I was puzzled by her choice: it was with my siblings that she had communicated most often. I wondered about her instinct to call me—whether it was out of some intimacy she'd felt, or something entirely different. Perhaps, having been in closer contact with my brother and sisters, she had not dared inform them.

At the funeral, the young woman looked timid and out of place, as if she feared her presence might upset us. Afterward I overheard her telling a neighbor that it had been a very peaceful passing. She hadn't said so to us, or perhaps we hadn't listened. There had been a full moon the night before, the young woman continued, and it was still visible at the hour of our mother's death. I felt a twinge of annoyance at her, both because she had witnessed my mother's last hours and because the information she retained was nevertheless worthless, incapable of adding any meaning to the loss or easing its pain.

THE HOUSE WAS sold within weeks. For several years our older brother had been alerting us to the growth in the region and the rising prices of real estate in the area. He had even suggested putting the house on the market so that we could move our mother to a comfortable facility where she would be taken care of round the clock. I had protested, and one of my sisters had been hesitant, and so we never brought up the topic with our mother. Now the house would be demolished to build a luxury hotel.

THE DAYS WERE rainy. I made tea and toast in the mornings and brought it to the living room, its walls stained with the outlines left behind by furniture and frames, unmoved for decades until the previous week. I sat in the wicker chair, looking out at the sodden garden overgrown with weeds. The roses had withered, chairs were knocked over on the grass. Still, I could feel some of my mother's presence here, where she had sat for hours. Only now was I able to understand that there had been serenity beneath her immobile gaze.

Come on, I would tell her, in my panic to bring her back to attention, to daily life, *let's go outside*. Or, *Mama, what are you thinking about?* I might turn on the radio, or pretend to laugh at something I'd just remembered. Anything to snap her out of her state. My attempts, of course, had been futile, and my mother continued to slip away.

When, toward the end of my stay, the sun appeared, I went out to collect the chairs and various discarded objects the movers had ignored. The air was soft; great white clouds moved across the sky. I decided I would have lunch in the garden once I had cleared the fallen branches and debris to one corner and given the grass a cursory rake. I found rusted tools in the garden shed—also untouched by the movers and my siblings. After I had tidied the branches, I set to work on the bushes, pulling out weeds to give the roses some space to breathe.

It wasn't until several hours later, when I went inside for a glass of water, that I realized the uselessness of my work: everything, not just the house but the garden, too, would be demolished in the coming months. Still, I went back outside, determined to clean up the flower beds at the far end, where at one time hollyhocks, primroses, irises, and yarrow had bloomed with abandon.

I crouched down on the ground, my hands sorting through the layers of old leaves and twigs to find the soil. It was a familiar place, though it had once appeared vast and enchanted, and I had now grown to see its true proportions. I thought back to my childhood, when I would squat there, gazing at a galaxy of color, believing that it contained some magic I could unlock with my stare. Once, when my mother was sick, I had come here daily to cut flowers for her, my small hands barely grasping the garden shears.

I seemed to recall that my mother had been very ill, then, though I could not be sure that this was really the case. Perhaps it had been nothing more than a bad cold, but in my memory of that time, I was struck by terror that something would happen to her. Every afternoon I brought her a flower and placed it at her bedside, willing it to provide some comfort. Each of my offerings, once I brought them in from the garden, had seemed so frail, and I knew that I could do little to alleviate her illness, no matter how bright a flower I managed to find. It was a useless gesture, and yet I continued to cut the flowers day after day.

I would walk silently through the door of my mother's room, pausing a moment for my eyes to adjust to the shadowy shapes. My mother would be lying in bed, and she'd turn her head to look, her stare at first distant, before she recognized me and began pulling herself out of the thick, impenetrable fog. Somehow, each time, she summoned the energy to smile, and I knew that it was not some magic from the flower that brought it about but rather something arising from my mother herself. Some source deep within her I could not reach. I was at once awed by this well of strength and terrified that it might dry up.

Future Selves

Some years after we moved to the city, my husband and I started looking for an apartment to buy. We were renting a small place past the southern boulevard that marked the end of the historic neighborhoods. On weekends we'd usually take walks, always in the direction of the finer quarters that had first lured us to the city with their old-world charm. We lived on an unremarkable street, without cafés or shops. At the corner was a large glass building on whose steps teenagers congregated at every hour, smoking, laughing, playing music. Those with skateboards rode up and down the boulevard, dodging out of the way of old women who frowned at them. During our first year, we learned that the building was a youth center, founded by a journalist couple whose own daughter's suffering had gone unnoticed in the midst of the parents' careers.

We'd been happy in our flat. At the time we moved in, it presented itself as a perfect space to play out our still elusive adulthoods. We bought oil paintings from flea markets, distinguishing our new home from the studio we'd lived in as graduate students, which we had decorated with framed posters. Now we had our sights set on a real kitchen, made of quality materials, a bathroom without chipped tiles or mold.

Our weekends, once taken up by those long walks, after which we would meet up with our friend Sami at a wine bar, were spent going from one end of the city to the other and sometimes out to the suburbs to look at apartments. More than the prospect of a home, we were intrigued by all the different lives, the arrangements of space to work and rest, to store and display, the priorities of strangers that were so different from our own. We still met up with Sami, and reported our finds to him over drinks that extended to dinners of cheeses and cured meats.

During our first weeks of searching we were struck by an eighteenth-century apartment, even smaller than our current one. It was impeccably restored, with an open kitchen fitted tastefully and resourcefully and a bathroom that, though tiny, gave the feeling of luxury. The owner was a flamboyant man in his fifties, whose exquisite belongings seemed to have been bought specifically to fit the shelves of his home. After showing us in, he took his place in a leather armchair and let us walk through the apartment ourselves, aware that it needed no explanation. Afterward my husband and I sat at a café down the street, with a red lacquered facade and marble tables. If we were to buy the apartment, we said, we'd come here for morning coffee and late-night drinks, would know the waiters by name. The thought was pleasing, though somewhat foreign, as if we'd put on very expensive clothing that didn't belong to us. Still, I could imagine us in this life tailored to perfection, like strangers I'd wish to befriend. When we showed Sami pictures of the apartment, he said it seemed ideal for a couple who received no guests and had no children. That part, he added, was for us to decide.

Another place that interested us was a loft in an old factory building. It was on the train line east, past the wealthy suburbs. After leaving the station, we had to cross a highway before arriving at an area of industrial lots, some abandoned, some converted into chic homes for young families, others occupied by immigrants. There was a mosque, and next to it a basketball court with a looming mural of Muhammad Ali. On the evening of our visit, lanky boys were throwing a ball with casual focus, calling out from time to time to their friends passing by. At the entrance of the mosque stood a man the size of a small child, with a thickly furrowed forehead, greeting those arriving for evening prayers.

Inside the gates of the converted factory was another world altogether. The walls were overgrown with green, the communal garden dotted with terra-cotta pots and round tables. The owners of the loft had three children, with toys made exclusively of wood. There were bicycles stacked against one wall, part of a cheerful clutter that communicated sanity and care. When we arrived, the family was cooking together, the children standing on stools, chopping and peeling with their small hands. I wondered whether the scene had been planned to coincide with our visit, though they were all so merry and welcomed us so warmly. The place was spacious enough that my husband and I could each have a work area and even host guests without having to change our routine. Our families lived in other countries, which was why this seemed an especially important prospect to consider.

After the visit, we could find no café in the neighborhood at which to sit and talk about our impressions, so we took the train back. On the way, we both said that we'd liked the diversity of the area, and would be excited to live there, though it also seemed that we might not be able to become part of the community, that we'd be living shuttered within the confines of the splendid loft, traveling all the way to the city whenever we went out. Over drinks the following evening, Sami told us he'd take the train to visit us on weekends. He was such a good friend to us, always offering his support of our choices.

Our parents asked if our creative work was secure enough for us to take on a mortgage, and wondered about the schools in the two neighborhoods and the availability of doctors, especially pediatricians, even though my husband and I had never said that we wanted to have children. We'd never denied the possibility, either. It was one of the aspects of our lives that we still needed to bring into focus, so that we could better picture a future home. The process was an act of imaginary acrobatics, trying to launch ourselves forward with only a guess at where we wanted to land.

AROUND THIS TIME, I went to visit my cousin Tara at her university. I took an early-morning flight, then caught the train to my cousin's campus, where I arrived in time for Halloween celebrations. My cousin had insisted that I come on that date, though I was a bit daunted by the idea of being at a party with students who were more than a decade younger than me. Tara met me at the station in a long, checkered wool coat that had once been mine. Her hair was bleached at the tips, and she was wearing makeup, which I'd never seen on her before. I noticed her pleasure at being autonomous in her new setting. She showed me the main street with its bookshops and cafés, an Italian restaurant and a bakery, as if the street were playing house.

Tara had made a dinner reservation, which moved me; I'd always been the one to take her out. When she came to visit us in the city—trips for her birthday, to celebrate her good grades in school—she'd felt like, if not exactly our child, then something close to it. After dinner we headed to her house, where some students were immersed in hysterical preparations, putting on makeup in the corridor, pouring drinks. One guy, trying to pull a tutu up to his waist, turned to give Tara a high five.

"Where's the gang?" Tara asked. The guy said that everyone was on their way.

We put my bag in Tara's room, which was lit with fairy lights and smelled sweetly of incense and weed.

"You'll sleep here," she said, though I'd offered to book a hotel in town. "And I'll stay with Mari."

Mari, beautiful and goofy, was part of the "gang," which had formed the previous semester, pulling all-nighters together during exams. Another member was an artistic kid named Luis. I guessed that Tara had a crush on him, because she acted exceedingly sisterly with him. The boy in the tutu and his twin brother had happily adopted the role of comic relief. There was Ellie, soft-spoken, and a guy named Simon, who I only later realized was part of the gang, after he'd accompanied us from party to party, finding the girls' coats for them amid the piles stacked high on beds when it was time to leave. I joined the group for a few hours—Tara and I had dressed up as fortune-tellers—then went back to Tara's room while the others went to a club downtown.

The following day, I read at a café while Tara was in class. I sent my husband a photograph of the narrow street, the students in sweatshirts, and texted that I'd been to more than one Halloween party the night before.

Shall we just move into a dorm? he wrote back.

In the evening I told Tara that I wanted to take her and her friends out to dinner. Tara objected at first, then conceded to inviting only two friends, because she didn't want me to pay "an avalanche bill."

"We should definitely invite Luis," I told her and winked, at which she smacked my arm. And Mari, I added. Later, as we were waiting to meet up with them in front of Tara's house, we saw Simon across the street. He walked over, looking for a moment as if he didn't remember who I was or, rather, as if I might not remember him—a look of apology.

"What're you ladies up to this fine evening?" he said, so awkwardly that I quickly asked him to join us. We went to the Italian restaurant on the main street. I ordered a bottle of wine and appetizers for us to share before our main courses of pasta.

"Could we just get the garlic bread?" Tara asked.

"Sure," I said. "I'm such an old woman. I don't know what you youngsters like to eat."

It was self-deprecation, of course. I knew I was young enough for them to consider me interesting. Tara had told me as much that morning—that her friends thought I was cool. I'd been strangely pleased by the compliments of twenty-year-olds. But I was old enough to have a direction in life, or so it seemed from the vantage point of Tara and her friends. They asked me about the city, and what it had taken for my husband and me to find our creative footing, to make a living from our passions. In turn, I asked them where they wanted to settle in the future, what they'd want to see from their bedroom windows. Mari and Tara led the conversation, discussing the advantages of living on a southern coast, where they could go swimming every morning, or on a rough western one where they could watch the crashing waves; perhaps they wanted to move to an exotic capital. Luis made fun of these options, which he called unpractical.

"Don't be so cynical," Tara said.

Luis brought his hand to his heart. " 'Tread softly because you tread on my dreams,' " he quoted.

"He's just showing off to you," Mari told me. "We're reading Yeats in lit class."

Simon was sitting at the far end of the table and didn't speak very much, but he laughed at whatever the others said. From time to time I asked him if there was anything else he wanted to order, though we'd more or less got everything on the menu.

On our way back, we were caught in a sudden downpour and took shelter in a doorway, water crashing down in front of us. We stood huddled, watching the street of identical three-story houses, smeared orange by the streetlights. After a while Luis and Mari said they would brave the rain, because they had to help their housemates set up for another party. They dashed off, holding their coats above their heads. When the rain finally slowed down, Simon walked home with us, then went to join the others. I hadn't realized that he'd stayed behind only to accompany us.

On my last morning, Tara and I had breakfast at the station café. I said that her friends were all wonderful. "I'm so happy you think so," Tara said, beaming. She admitted that she did like Luis, as I'd guessed, but felt that Mari did as well. She and Mari were already so competitive, and she didn't want to jeopardize the friendship. I hadn't picked up on the competition; perhaps I still perceived Tara in her childish innocence. Her eyes clouded for a moment, the way they used to in her childhood, when she heard the slightest note of tension at a family gathering. Then she smiled. "Oh, never mind, it's so silly." She went on to tell me about the twin brothers, who, she said, were actually really smart.

"What's the story with Simon?" I asked. Tara said he was a really nice guy, perhaps the only balanced one in their group of weirdos. He always listened to their dramas without judgment, never took sides in arguments. I could tell that it pleased her to consider herself weird, the way it had pleased me at her age, providing an identity that cloaked the shakier aspects of myself that I didn't want to confront.

When my plane landed that evening, I saw that Tara had posted photos of the two of us from Halloween, and from the Italian restaurant, as well as a final selfie we'd taken before I boarded the train. Our faces looked so similar that they might have been a time roll of a single life.

IT WASN'T UNTIL the following year that my husband and I finally made an offer on an apartment. We'd broadened our search all around the city and suburbs, then narrowed it again. We came to realize that we wouldn't feel at home living in a faraway neighborhood. Nor did it seem right to move into a small and beautiful apartment where we would live as if embalmed, receiving no visitors, and have no room for a child, if that was what we wanted. I'd found out, after an ultrasound to investigate some abdominal pains, that my chances of conceiving were somewhat low. It was nothing serious, the doctor assured me, though it might be important for us to start trying, if we wished to have a family. I'd always considered the phrase puzzling—having a family—since we already had a family, indeed several. I didn't understand why our lives should be deemed lacking.

Tara and her gang had moved into a shared house. On a video call, Tara showed me the gray-carpeted floors, the utilitarian kitchen and bathroom. Over text messages that semester, she told me that she and Luis had had a brief thing. I didn't ask what this meant, feeling that I should respect her privacy, though I would certainly have asked a friend about the physical and emotional aspects of the affair. It had petered out, Tara wrote, sort of, and now it looked as if Luis and Mari were going to get together. I assumed that these texts were distilled from what must have been a constant turmoil in their lives, of heartbreaks and misunderstandings, swapped loyalties, conversations analyzed to shreds with new friends, making strangers become family within a matter of days. Still, I was happy to follow the developments in Tara's life, albeit from a distance.

I sent her pictures of different apartments, including some we'd decided against but which were more interesting than the practical ones we were seriously considering. Tara wrote back to tell me which window nook or bedroom she would claim and asked whether she could live with us for a year after graduation to write her novel. This was something she used to predict for her future—that she would live in a romantic city, working on a book. At one time I, too, had talked with certainty about all the things I'd do in the future—wildly different projects that would somehow all materialize—as if I had already attained them without even trying.

•

THE APARTMENT WE finally chose was in the opposite direction from our city walks, though not so far that we lived out of reach of the beautiful neighborhoods. It was on an unremarkable street, in a modern building without any flourishes. Inside were straight corners and clean countertops, closets that were nothing beyond their mere function. But there was a spare bedroom, which we could use as an office, and later, perhaps, for a crib. Sami told us that we'd made a great decision; the apartment really suited us. He was being encouraging, though I found it insulting that he thought the bland place matched our tastes. Still, once we hung up our paintings and softened corners with plants, the apartment would come alive, would indeed begin to look more like the image of ourselves that we envisioned.

We sent our parents photos on the day of our move, boxes piled all around the living room. I wrote to Tara that she should come after her midterm exams for the housewarming party. She didn't respond, which wasn't unusual; she was often busy with school and overwhelmed by the threads of conversation on her phone, with friends in her immediate life and those far away. A few days later, I sent her a photo of the desk we'd set up in the spare room.

So lovely, Tara wrote back.

Waiting for someone to write a novel, I responded, and asked how things were going.

All right, Tara said, adding that she and her housemates were worried about a friend of theirs who hadn't come home since the weekend. His family hadn't heard from him, nor had his classmates. Tara and her housemates were probably his closest friends, and they had no idea, either.

Which friend is this? I asked.

Simon.

It took me a moment to remember who he was; his name hadn't appeared in Tara's updates in the past months.

I told her I was sorry. I hoped Simon would get in touch soon. I remembered something that had happened at my university, which I hadn't thought about in years. I hadn't known the boy very well, but I used to exchange daily greetings with him at the library where he and I had adjacent research stalls. He'd left a party one snowy night and was found more than a week later, too late. No one knew what had happened—whether he was drunk, or troubled, or something else.

WITHIN WEEKS, WE were settled. We hired an electrician to install wiring in the ceiling so we could hang a green lamp, Sami's housewarming present, above the dining table. We went on walks in our neighborhood, always picking a different direction, to identify the places we would frequent, impatient for the time when we would blend in with our surroundings and could claim a history in our new home.

It wasn't from Tara but from her mother that I heard the rest of the story. Tara had come home following Simon's disappearance, taking time off from school because she wanted to be with her parents. On the phone, my aunt told me that the housemates had found a note in the kitchen a few days after he went missing; it had somehow ended up in the recycling box, though it must initially have been left in a conspicuous spot. By then, the police had already searched the local area and weren't hopeful. In his note, Simon said that he couldn't see a place for himself in the world. Not the way that others did. All around him, he wrote, were people who knew what they wanted, and where they belonged.

One of the terrible shocks, my aunt told me, was that no one had even caught a hint of what was happening, at least not until the aftermath. "God help that family," my aunt said. "God give them patience." I'd never heard her speak like this, and her words chilled me.

After we hung up, I thought of the dinner at the Italian restaurant, going over the questions I'd asked everyone about how they wanted their lives to turn out. Of course, it was unreasonable for me to feel guilty about the situation, as if I'd been responsible for forcing Simon to confront the impossibility of imagining a future that would accommodate him. I wondered whether Tara had also gone over that conversation in her mind, though she must have had many more memories of Simon than the single one from which I tried to glean meaning.

But it wasn't so much this I thought about for the rest of the afternoon as it was the fact that Tara hadn't called to tell me what had happened. I wished she'd asked to come and stay with us for a while, or at least turned to me for consolation. At the same time, I chided myself for longing for Tara's attention at such a moment. As I went about my day, I thought uneasily that the event would eventually make us distant; that our intimacy had now come to an end, as had Tara's carefree youth. Perhaps Tara would grow to despise that youth, would perceive in it her own obliviousness.

I'd always been proud that Tara looked up to me, wanted to live as I did, in a beautiful city, with a partner whose tastes and interests mirrored her own, even though I knew that such admiration would inevitably expire. Still, I'd delighted in my cousin's childish esteem. Ridiculous as it may be, I found in it a validation of my own life.

When my husband came home that evening, I didn't share any of this with him; there was nothing tangible in my worries. I'd let my mind hurtle ahead to scenarios in which Tara became a stranger to me. I told my husband only what had happened to Simon.

We were sitting at the dining table, our hands almost touching beneath the warm pool of the light, waiting for the water on the stove to boil. I said that the trajectory of events—from Simon's even keel when we first met, all the way up to the note—felt like something out of a film. Perhaps, though, I had exaggerated Simon's calm demeanor in my retelling, having no other details to offer from my brief visit. In any case, I was aware that the lives of strangers appeared improbable only because they were seen from a distance.

The living room windows had fogged up with steam, and my husband got up to turn off the stove. There were sounds coming from the upstairs flat; our neighbors must have been throwing a party. It was a constant, lively hum, pierced now and then by a higher pitch.

Freedom to Move

I was in Istanbul for a few days on my way to visit my grandfather. He'd moved in with my father at the beginning of the pandemic because we were worried about him living alone, in the town by the Black Sea where he'd retired. We'd urged him to come to the city, just for a short time. It was a wise decision; my grandfather's health deteriorated rapidly in those months, and his stay became indefinite. He could no longer go out for long walks as he used to, or even remain upright for extended periods.

My grandfather had always spent his days outdoors. Whenever he came to Istanbul, he'd take buses and ferries all over the city, sometimes going as far as the city's gates. He traveled around the country with a tent. He stayed in mountain villages and invited himself to breakfast at the homes of locals. He loved that sort of thing—meeting strangers, seeing different lives. He often urged us, his grandchildren, to join him. He showed us pictures of the people he'd met on these trips, with whom he kept in touch. One time, when I was having breakfast with him at a seaside café in Istanbul, a boy of ten or eleven video-called to wish him a happy *bayram*.

"Come again soon, Grandpa," the boy said.

My cousins and I all lived abroad, and we found it difficult to set aside time for such travels; our visits back home consisted of seeing many people in a short span. But we were proud of our grandfather—his youthful spirit and his sense of adventure. Perhaps we felt that it indicated something about us as well, something like a family identity.

Since my arrival, I had seen relatives and friends, and had also been to the Bosphorus, Moda, and Cihangir—outings that had always signified a proper visit back, though I could no longer say that I enjoyed them. The neighborhoods changed rapidly between my trips, and they were so crowded. The city was packed beyond belief, filled with tourists—a thick stream of people moving slowly, engulfing everything. I felt resentment toward them, and I longed for the city where I'd grown up.

I had phoned my grandfather the night before to tell him I would visit the following afternoon. Had I called sooner, he would have asked me to come straightaway and planned meals together throughout my stay. My father was going to be out when I went over. He had a few things to do, he told me, and besides, he preferred to spend time alone with me rather than see me with my grandfather. This wasn't very convenient, but I sensed that the living arrangement had begun to take its toll. It now seemed inconceivable that my grandfather would be able to go back to his small town. Of course my father never mentioned any of this, but I gathered from phone conversations that he was out more and more. Later that afternoon I would meet him for coffee before going to my mother's for dinner with my aunts. It was exhausting to be home, to feel torn between obligations because of our fractured family.

I'd just got into the taxi when my grandfather called to ask where I was.

"I'm on my way," I told him, "but it will take me some time to get there." I could picture his impatience. He must have gotten dressed hours ago. He would have been looking out the window, scouting for my arrival. He called again as the taxi was crossing the bridge. He'd forgotten to tell me that the downstairs buzzer didn't always work, so I should press hard when I got there. Then he called a third time to say I should just phone as I was approaching.

"Granddad," I said, a little flustered. "I'll see you soon."

•

AT THE DOOR I was greeted by the woman my father had hired to help around the house after my grandfather moved in. I'd met her once before, and it came back to me now that she was Georgian, though I couldn't immediately remember her name.

"Grandfather is very impatient today," she said. She spoke Turkish with a thick accent, emphasizing words in unexpected ways, but I found it remarkable that she already had such a command of the language.

I took off my shoes and coat, then went into the living room, where my grandfather was sitting in an armchair. He made a move to get up, but I motioned to him to stay put and kissed his cheeks. He was terribly gaunt. Little flakes of dead skin stuck to his forehead. Still, he was wearing a three-piece suit and tie, doubtless for my sake.

"Look at you," I said. "Look at this handsome gentleman."

I sat across from him, recounting my first days in Istanbul, the people I'd seen so far. I told him that my mother had cooked an extraordinary dish of lamb on my arrival.

"She never comes to visit," my grandfather said. "And she hasn't invited me over since I moved here."

I was glad my mother wasn't there to hear this; I felt at once angered and saddened by my grandfather's wish to be hosted by his former daughter-in-law.

"She's working," I told him. "She barely has a minute to herself." I didn't have the heart to explain that my mother had no desire to see my father's family, let alone serve them.

Ketevan—I now recalled her name—was standing in the doorway and asked when we would like to eat.

I told her that I wasn't very hungry. I'd just pour myself a cup of tea. If my grandfather wanted something, I could prepare him a tray. But as I said this, I noticed that the dining table was set as if for a New Year's meal, with a white tablecloth and red napkins, a vase of carnations.

"Of course you're going to eat," my grandfather said. "We'll eat all together."

Someone else had appeared behind Ketevan, a teenage girl, maybe fifteen years old.

"Little Princess is here," my grandfather said.

Although the table was set for four, Ketevan kept on repeating that she and Natela—her daughter—could eat in the kitchen.

"Please sit with us," I told her. At the same time, I was annoyed that my grandfather had come up with such a plan, had made the woman cook and asked that we all eat together. *Surely*, I thought, *the mother and daughter would rather be by themselves.*

"I asked her to make you her specialties," my grandfather said.

He motioned to me to help him get up, and we walked step by step to the table, his hand resting heavily on my arm. Again, I took in how frail he'd become, and I couldn't quite believe it, as if his old self were concealed within this approximation of my grandfather. I had the irrational feeling that this was just a phase, and he would soon be restored to vitality.

It was awkward to be sitting at the table while Natela and Ketevan brought dishes, so I got up to help them. In the kitchen was a tray of golden buns, a salad of grated carrots and one of beets, and a cake, decorated with sliced fruits.

"This is too much," I told Ketevan. "You really shouldn't have."

She shook her head and smiled at me, then handed me a plate of food to carry.

OVER LUNCH I asked Natela questions, and her mother translated her answers. She'd arrived in Istanbul three months ago; she was now working at an office across the street. Already she could understand much of what was said, but she was still shy about responding in Turkish.

"What do you do at the office?" I asked, and her mother told me that it was mostly cleaning and cooking. Natela was not as young as I'd guessed—she'd finished high school last summer.

"Do you like Istanbul?" I asked.

Natela shrugged. She said something to her mother. Then she told me, in English, "I like Taksim Square. But Mama doesn't like it."

"Your English is very good," I said. I repeated the same in Turkish to Ketevan, who beamed with pride. She said that Taksim was an awful place; there was no knowing what sort of people hung out there.

Natela was wearing a tight black dress. There were stacks of bracelets on her wrists. Below her left elbow was a small tattoo in the shape of a bird. *She was so young*, I thought, *and so impatient to mature*. I could guess at her tilt toward desire, toward freedom.

The summer I graduated from high school, I was out around Taksim with my friends every day, returning home late at night. I'd been accepted by a prestigious university abroad, and I allowed myself every caprice, something my parents indulged. I felt sorry for Natela, that she had to sit around with us. She must find this all so boring.

"Why doesn't she go now?" I suggested. "It's still early, and she has the day off."

"If you want to go," Ketevan said, "you can go."

Natela nuzzled her face against her mother's arm.

"We made a cake," she said.

I saw then that she was also still a child.

"Is our boy full?" Ketevan asked. She handed my grandfather another roll, then served him more of the colorful salads. "When your father is around, Grandfather's diet is very strict. No dessert, no bread. Meat to feed a bird. But our boy loves to eat. Let him enjoy himself."

"I guess so," I said.

"After all," she added, "what else does he have to look forward to?"

I was startled by her bluntness and quickly changed the subject, even though my grandfather didn't seem to mind. Whenever I talked to him on the phone, I made sure to tell him that he would soon be strong enough to go out for walks, and that he should prepare to dance with me at a relative's wedding in Ayvalık that summer.

My grandfather had started on his second plate and looked over to see if I was eating.

"Kezban is a great cook," he said.

"*Ketevan*," I corrected.

"Kezban's my name for her. She's Kezban, and Little Princess is Nihal."

"Granddad, you can't just make up names."

"We don't mind," Ketevan said.

I told her that I'd been to Georgia once, a few years earlier, with my then boyfriend.

"Oh?"

"You have a beautiful country," I said, knowing that this was a cliché. I was often told the same thing by people who'd visited Turkey, and then had to listen to a list of the obvious sights they'd seen. Still, I also named the places we'd traveled to—Tbilisi, Batumi, a day trip to Mtskheta.

"Very good," Ketevan said. "A very good trip."

"When was the last time you were home?"

She and Natela had been back a few months ago, she said, just as soon as the travel restrictions were lifted, though there were still firm measures in place. On top of this, my father had allowed her only a ten-day holiday, which meant that by the time they'd traveled there and spent a week in confinement, the visit was almost over. They'd barely seen their relatives; on the one day they could go outside, they had managed to take flowers to Ketevan's mother's grave.

It occurred to me that I actually knew about this trip: my father hadn't been able to find a replacement for Ketevan during her absence. He'd had to spend the whole time at home, helping my grandfather.

"Going off like that and leaving me in the middle of this," he'd complained on the phone. "Your grandfather's impossible. He's literally looking for ways to get injured."

My father was increasingly short-tempered with his father. He was aggrieved when my grandfather disobeyed the smallest rules—eating sweets, or not using both hands to steady himself when he got up from his armchair.

"Where did you stay when you went back?" I asked Ketevan.

"At our home," she said. "With my husband and son." She told me the name of a town, and though I nodded, I'd never heard of it.

She and her husband had built this house, she explained, across from her in-laws, with whom they shared an orchard. Her own siblings used to live a short distance away. That life was gone now. There was no work for any of them. Her brother was in Spain, her sister in Azerbaijan. Her son was also trying to move, perhaps to join her and Natela in Istanbul. Her in-laws had passed away recently. But at least her husband still tended to the orchard. They had many fruit trees; they grew grapes.

She said something to Natela, nudging her.

From the kitchen, Natela brought a plastic bottle, wrapped in cellophane.

"My husband's wine," Ketevan announced. She took the bottle from her daughter and started to unwrap it.

"Oh, no," I said, "you should drink that yourself. It's so special."

Ketevan continued unwrapping.

"I want to taste it," my grandfather said.

"Granddad," I said, "alcohol is terrible for you. Please don't," I told Ketevan. "Please don't open it for us."

"Today's a special day," Ketevan said.

"That's so kind, but there's no need," I insisted.

"A special day for us," Ketevan added. "It's Natela's name day."

I felt foolish for having assumed that the wine was an offering to me and my grandfather. I was also embarrassed that they had to spend the day in our company, and had made so many preparations.

"Why didn't you say so?" I said. It was still possible for Natela to leave, I repeated, and join her friends somewhere.

"Is a name day like a birthday? Do you have a party?"

"We celebrated this morning," Natela said. "Mama made the buns for breakfast. We lit a candle and prayed. We phoned home when Grandfather was sleeping."

Once again, I felt silly for thinking that all the food was in my honor. It seemed that my grandfather hadn't known about the name day, either, and that Ketevan and Natela had wanted to mark it privately.

Ketevan brought out crystal glasses from the buffet behind the dining table. I remembered that my parents had bought these glasses during a holiday in Slovenia. They were among the many objects that had become the bitter focus of their separation. Perhaps that was why I'd never seen my father use them. My mother, too, mostly avoided the possessions that she'd victoriously laid claim to.

Ketevan filled our glasses, halfway for my grandfather. Natela brought out the cake.

"Excellent," my grandfather said. "They have a very rich cuisine."

"What's the tradition?" I asked. "Do we sing a song?"

"We make toasts," Ketevan said.

I raised my glass. "To Natela's name day," I said. "May all her dreams come true."

The wine was sweet, and very strong.

Next, Ketevan raised her glass.

She spoke in Georgian, and Natela listened solemnly, her head bowed. Then, once again, she pressed her face against her mother's arm.

"I toast to her future," Ketevan said in Turkish. "Like you, I toast to her dreams. So that we may be together as a family, and we don't have to dream of things far away."

Of course, my toast had been a platitude, open-ended to accommodate any wish. Still, I might have imagined Natela dreaming of a future in Europe or America, one in which she would be traveling the world. At her age, I had wished only to be off, to be free, to start my life elsewhere.

Ketevan continued. "I toast that these times come to an end, and our countries can manage on their own. I toast," she said, "that people don't have to leave their homes."

My grandfather had finished his cake and started nodding off at the table.

"Granddad," I said, stroking his hand. "You're falling asleep."

"Big boy ate well," Ketevan said. She put down her glass, still full. We helped my grandfather get up and walked him step by step to his armchair.

It was the end of the toasts. Natela started stacking the plates. She screwed the cap back on the bottle and carried the cake to the kitchen.

Once he was seated, my grandfather motioned to the remote control, mumbling that there was a show about to start.

My father had texted to ask what time we would meet.

"I'll let you watch your show," I told my grandfather, but he was adamant that I sit down with him. He called out to Ketevan, who was clearing the table, to make tea.

"It's brewing," she said, perhaps a little brusquely.

The show, like so many others, was about the intrigues of a large and wealthy family. Each time a new character appeared onscreen, my grandfather supplied background information about illegitimate children, blackmail, matriarchal ploys. It was difficult to keep track of the series of complicated relationships that he'd mastered; the whole thing seemed outrageously far-fetched. Still, I feigned interest.

Once the table was cleared and the tea served, Natela also came to watch.

"Do you like this show?" I asked.

She shrugged. "I don't understand everything."

"I don't understand everything, either." I smiled.

Every fifteen minutes, the show was interrupted by commercials.

"A single episode must take the whole day," I told my grandfather.

"All the better for me," he said. "At least it fills the time."

I felt sad that he'd said this, and so openly. I thought I should've arranged some way to take him out, perhaps to sit by the Bosphorus or eat at a restaurant. Still, I had to leave soon to see my father before dinner. I was hoping that my grandfather would fall asleep and I could slip out, but he was now alert, watching even the commercials with interest.

"Granddad," I said, putting my hand on his, "I should get going."

"What's the rush?"

I told him I was going to see my father.

"Why doesn't he come home?"

"I think he had a meeting," I mumbled.

"Very well," my grandfather said.

"I'll try to come again before I leave. But if I can't, remember that you have to prepare your dance moves for the wedding."

"Very well," my grandfather said again. "Say hello to your mother."

I was taken aback by his curt farewell, as if his resignation were also a sign of his physical state, evidence of my altered grandfather.

"I'm going to try to visit once more," I repeated. "I'll let you know."

I knelt down and kissed his cheeks. Then I kissed them again, and stroked the wisps of combed hair on his scalp.

DURING THE COMMERCIAL break, Natela had joined her mother in the kitchen and was sitting on a stool, chatting merrily, while Ketevan washed the stack of pans and trays. Natela sprang to her feet when she saw me at the door.

"I have to get going," I said. "Thank you for an amazing lunch."

Ketevan put aside a heavy casserole and wiped her hands on her apron.

"It's still early," she said. "Grandfather was so excited to see you."

I felt anger toward her, and shame.

"It's difficult to see everyone properly on such a short visit."

Natela had fetched my coat and held it open for me to put on.

"Happy name day, Natela," I said. "And thank your father for his delicious wine."

As I was putting on my shoes, Ketevan asked if I could talk to my father: she wanted to go back home in the spring. She'd already asked my father two times, but he'd been very firm. She'd known from the beginning what the work entailed, he told her; she could take it or leave it.

She didn't want to anger him, Ketevan said, but it was important for her to see her family.

"I haven't asked him for a raise all year," she said. "And Natela always helps out with Grandfather after work. He's so happy when she's around. She brings him joy."

I was nodding the entire time that she spoke, even though I felt that I didn't have any say in these matters. I told her that I would mention it to my father.

•

IT WAS SUNNY outside, bustling with traffic, pedestrians, street sellers: the heart of the day. I walked toward Barbaros Boulevard, where I'd hail a cab. I'd more or less decided that I wasn't going to mention Ketevan's request to my father. No doubt it would only anger him once again, and I didn't want to spoil our short time together. Anyway, I was in no position to defend the woman, to explain her wish to see her husband and son. I was leaving in a few days, free of responsibilities; I wasn't the one overseeing my grandfather's daily needs. Besides, I didn't want my grandfather to be left with some stranger in the weeks that Ketevan and Natela would be gone; he was so comfortable in the mother and daughter's company. Surely they could go back in the summer, when my grandfather traveled with us to the wedding.

I thought about writing to my cousins that evening on our WhatsApp group, to plan a trip following the wedding in Ayvalık. Our chat history consisted mostly of funny things we'd come across online, as well as childhood photos we unearthed during our visits back. I would suggest taking our grandfather to a hotel or a holiday rental. Granddad loved the sea, and he'd loved to swim. Barely two years ago, he'd gone swimming in the middle of autumn, proudly telling us how much good the cold water did the body and the mind. We could find a place on the coast, a house without stairs. He would sit and watch the sea. I had an image of all of us gathered around him on a terrace, pressing him for stories we hadn't heard before or hadn't paid attention to. *For one thing*, I thought, *we should ask him about all the trips he had made around Turkey sleeping in a tent, and the strangers he'd met.*

On Barbaros Boulevard, I stood with my hand raised, waiting for a cab. I tried to put aside the nagging feeling that my grandfather might not make it to the wedding.

Where are you? my father texted. *Let me know if you're still planning on meeting.*

I ignored his tone of annoyance and wrote that I was on my way, but I wouldn't be able to stay for very long.

Cry It Out

For a long time, all we talked about was the baby's sleep. When friends and relatives asked us for updates, we would list the ways in which we were exhausted, in a desperate attempt to make them understand: the baby could only nap if he was in our arms. He cried every few hours and had to be rocked back to sleep. He woke up for the day at six in the morning, sometimes at five.

Before the birth, my friend Anna had given me a book about baby sleep. It was the only one I needed to read, she assured me.

"Just take my word for it," she said. "This book is the one that works."

Anna's son, Luca, was long past the age of constant care, but the advice of the book remained solid, she said.

She had given the book to several other mothers, and they had all been grateful.

At the time I'd thanked Anna for the gift, though I thought that I would not really need it. I'd always been a little patronizing toward the difficulties of parents. Before the baby, I'd more or less thought that if only mothers were more relaxed, the problems of their children would smoothly unknot.

In the weeks following the birth, my husband skimmed the book and summarized its main point: a baby needed to learn how to sleep on its own. The ability to soothe oneself to sleep, the author claimed, was a learned skill, just like eating with a fork or putting on shoes. According to the book, though, our baby was still too young to train, because it involved letting the baby cry. In those days, when time expanded to monstrous scales, each day a trial of our endurance, it seemed that we would never get to the mark, only a few months away, when we would be permitted to carry out the training. We'd heard from other friends that we could start a week or two earlier if the baby showed signs of maturity. They added that it would take some courage on our end. Courage? we joked. Our nerves were so frayed that we would have done anything for a calm evening, a few hours of uninterrupted sleep.

A WAR BROKE out on the other side of the world on the baby's four-month birthday.

That morning we had dressed him in a flannel shirt and trousers, though he normally spent all day in pajamas. We didn't read the news of the war until a few days later, and even then we had little idea of the scale of events. We didn't really have time to think about anything but the immediate requirements of our days. My husband had gone back to work, albeit with shortened hours. I greeted him each afternoon with an outpouring of despair. We couldn't continue like this, I said. We needed to make a change.

"I know," he told me. "Soon we'll start the training."

Friends came by to bring us food and stay for tea, or go on a walk with the baby strapped to them, hopping him up and down so he would fall asleep. When we asked them on these visits how they were doing, they would shrug solemnly and say something vague, like "You know," or "It's a strange time."

"What happened?" we asked. "Is everything all right?"

After a few times, it became clear that they were all referring to the war. It seemed important to state right away that it was on their minds. Some of them, realizing we'd been more or less unaware of the debates, were restless to tell us their version of events. The war defined something about them, something about their worldview as well as how they were viewed in the world.

In other wars, our friends had come together in solidarity. We had organized fundraisers, attended protests, volunteered at organizations. Just the previous year, we had all gathered in the home of Anna for a classical music concert to benefit two young artists who had escaped active combat in their hometown. At the end of the evening, Anna's young son Luca had played a pop song on his guitar while his parents collected contributions. The family invited the artists to stay with them for a month while they applied for asylum. We had applauded our friends for their generosity, though it turned out that the young artists had been disruptive, drinking with their friends until the late hours of the night. A shame, we said, when Anna and her husband had been so generous.

Our friend Aziz was the only one to point out that a space to congregate with alcohol was the best gift to offer young refugees. Aziz was a peripheral figure in our circle. We never knew whether he would show up and how long he might stay. But his presence was always welcome—he smoked too much and drank with joy; he gave every conversation his full attention. That he'd known hardships far greater than any of us legitimized our gatherings and made them feel that much more worthwhile. In the end, Anna had been forced to ask the artists to leave, because Luca's schedule was disturbed by the commotion in their household: he went to bed late on weeknights, woke up tired for school. We agreed that it was an inevitable decision.

This war loosened the bonds of our community. Some argued that it was more complicated—the oppressors were not so evil as we had thought unanimously of the oppressors of all previous wars. They were our brothers, after all; a people so similar to us in every way. Others said that to forgive sins in our own image was a greater evil than any other. Others still were committed to silence—if they cared, one way or another, they were more worried about what their caring might cost them. My husband and I were now fully abreast of the war—its facts and justifications, arguments and counterarguments—and we stood, startled, in its crossfire.

Aziz was over one Saturday for a drink. He'd brought a bottle of whisky and a bag of chips, so different from our other visitors who arrived with chicken stock and casseroles. We hadn't seen Aziz since the birth, though he seemed unaware that our lives had changed dramatically. It was refreshing not to be treated as tired parents; it gave us energy.

The baby had been fussy that day, refusing to nap, and we took turns rocking him, while Aziz poured drinks.

"So, how have you guys been?" Aziz asked.

We told him about our battles with sleep, and about the method of letting the baby cry.

"Huh," Aziz said. "Sounds pretty barbaric." He added that he knew nothing about the topic; we'd probably already discussed it with other parents.

My husband asked whether he'd been in touch with our mutual friends.

"Not really. Everyone's holed up, shouting their opinions, selecting their slice of humanity."

It was strange, he continued, to live in the same city, in the same neighborhoods, and make ourselves heard on our social media accounts. It revealed that we were scared of one another, that we were strangers at heart.

I wanted to ask him what he thought about the war, trusting that his opinion would be true, and direct, but the baby had started crying.

"Close your eyes, baby," I murmured. "Aziz thinks drinking is more honest than clever arguments. And he thinks you're in for it with your upcoming training."

This was a game we played, my husband and I, to resist the mindless babble of baby-speak. Neither of us knew any lullabies, either, so we talked, our voices hushed and sweet, and we discovered that in recounting the immediate events of our lives to the baby, we often hit upon their essential aspects.

AS THE DATE for the training drew closer, my husband and I read the book more carefully. The baby still woke up very early in the morning, though he no longer cried as frequently as he used to. Sometimes we even managed to put him down in his cot for a nap. But at night he still slept with us. In fact, he would only fall asleep if we were on either side of him, our hands placed on his belly. There was something lovely about this, it was true, the three of us holding hands across the bed. Sometimes, when we all woke in the night for a feed, the baby would flash smiles from left to right, giddy with our presence. Perhaps we would even miss this time, once we'd forgotten.

The method was simple: we would feed the baby, kiss him good night, put him in his bed, and leave the room. It was assumed that he would then start crying, and we would have to wait, without intervening, until he fell asleep. He was bound to fall asleep, sooner or later. It was like this that babies learned: once they understood that their caregivers would not help them cross from wakefulness to slumber; when they knew that they had to make the passage on their own. The book added that while the method was perfectly safe, some babies might throw up from intense crying.

Anna wrote to us periodically, asking whether we had trained the baby. There was something pressing in her questions, as if she was impatient for us to do it, to put our baby through what they had. Not for our sake but for her own: a plea to join the community. For our child to know what theirs knew.

When the time came, she said, we would need to remain strong, and to remind ourselves why we were doing this.

HAD IT ALWAYS been the case that wars were reported through the suffering of children? Perhaps it was my own attuned state, the way I could imagine every stranger's face as an infant, could recognize in it my own baby's expressions. In the news, I saw only the amputated limbs and rubble-smeared faces of children. One night, unable to sleep after feeding the baby, though he had miraculously rolled back to a deep slumber without having to be rocked, I read about the bombing of a school where several thousand people had taken refuge. The photographs showed a crater that had once been a playground. The next image, which I hadn't prepared myself to see, was of a mother kneeling by the body of her child, her hands clasping the child's thin arms, as if trying to resuscitate her. I turned off my phone immediately and put my hand on the baby's belly, steadily rising and falling. I stroked his cheeks, hoping that I would wake him up and he'd smile.

OUR PARENTS PLEADED with us not to train our baby to sleep. A baby needed security, my mother insisted. It needed to be rocked and comforted. I was furious at her, so removed from the exhaustion of our days. She assured me that my sisters and I all woke up several times a night, and that we'd all been soothed for years.

"Years?" I exclaimed. "You want us to go on like this for *years*?" I couldn't quite believe that my siblings and I had ever caused so much trouble, and besides, there had been my grandmothers and aunts to help.

My husband's parents admitted that they had let their children cry until they fell asleep.

"But only a little bit," my father-in-law said. "It wasn't all night or anything like that." My mother-in-law added that she had never thought it a very good idea.

"We didn't know any better," she said. "That's just what people did back then."

We didn't tell our parents that just three days prior, the baby had started sleeping in his own room for the first few hours of the evening, after which we brought him to bed with us when he cried. It was a victory, when all we had wanted for months was an hour to ourselves in the evenings. But it quickly seemed like so little, and we were impatient to gain further territory.

ANNA WAS THROWING a birthday lunch for her son. The boy had done exceedingly well in his classes that year, and had won a nationwide poetry contest. His sonnet was displayed in various public transports. Friends had already spotted it on a bus, on the metro, even the tram. It would be "an afternoon of poetry," Anna informed us in an email, "a space of solace when there is so much sadness in the world."

Not all our friends, I noticed, were on the invite. Of the bits and pieces I gathered from our visitors, I guessed that these friends differed in opinion from Anna, who had been conspicuously quiet about the war. She'd confessed to one friend that she feared causing offense by "taking sides." What side was there to take, the friend later asked me in fury, when a whole nation was on the brink of starvation? Yet others, who had been invited, took offense at Anna's wording. It was pathetic to invoke solace as an excuse for the party.

You guys going to the poetry solace? Aziz texted my husband, who told him we were thinking about it.

It'll be good to get out of the house, he added. We'd never gone anywhere with the baby, save for walks in the neighborhood. Besides, it was unfair to blame Anna for her wording, to assume the worst. We told Aziz he should come, too. It would be great to see him.

I was happy to dress up, when I had spent months in baggy shirts and sweatpants. I wore a bright blue dress and gold earrings, small ones the baby couldn't tug at. My husband strapped him to his chest, and I carried the straw bassinet filled with gifts: a bottle of wine, a book about astronomy for Luca, pastries.

"It's so great to see you all," Anna told us at the door. The baby grinned at her, delighted. Anna had met him once before and commented now that he'd grown tremendously.

"Listen to me," she said, wagging her finger, "it's time to let your parents rest."

Then she opened her arms to me in an embrace. "You look lovely, and utterly exhausted."

I noticed with some unease that the usual crowd wasn't there; we hardly knew anyone at the party. Anna introduced me to a group standing around the buffet table.

"She came with her newborn," she said, pointing at my husband, who was rocking the baby in a corner of the room. "It's so special that they could be here."

I felt tension in her voice, an effort to preempt something I might say—though what it was, I didn't know.

She squeezed my arm. "Anyway," she said, "I'll leave you to enjoy yourself."

One of the men in the group asked if we were getting any sleep.

"Not really," I told him. "Do you have children?"

He pointed to the lanky teenage girl standing next to him in a knee-length dress and braces, holding her plate as if it were something very precious.

"Hello," the girl said politely, then turned to face the buffet table, which she picked at daintily, considering each food's position on her plate.

An equally lanky woman, the girl's mother, said that the first years were really tough.

"But you'll forget all about it," she said.

I asked whether their daughter had been a good sleeper.

"You know," the woman said, "she really wasn't that bad. We were lucky."

"So I guess you didn't have to sleep train?"

"Oh yes," the man said, "you have to do it."

Had they ever tried the method of letting the baby cry?

There was something like panic in the woman's face, as if I'd mentioned a great taboo.

She nodded her head imperceptibly, throwing a quick glance at her daughter, still arranging food on her plate.

"Only a few times," she mumbled.

I could hear the baby's crying from another room, where my husband must have retreated. I left the group and found him in Luca's bedroom, where guests had piled their coats. He'd placed the baby in the bassinet, and was trying to calm him by stroking his belly. The baby was crying desperately.

"He's really sleepy," my husband announced. "But he can't seem to manage on his own."

I took the baby in my arms and rocked him.

"We're at a party," I murmured. "It's a little boring here, but at least there's food. None of our other friends showed up, because they think the hosts are morally problematic."

Soon the baby's eyes began to close. When he was asleep, I sat with him by the pile of coats, and my husband crouched on the floor. The naps lasted only twenty minutes or so; it wasn't worth trying to put him down. Besides, it was nice to be the three of us. Now that we had finally left our neighborhood, I mostly wanted to be back home.

WHEN WE EMERGED from the bedroom, Anna was announcing that they would start the reading.

"Darling," she said, "we're all ready for you."

Without protest, Luca arrived in front of the buffet. He was wearing jeans and a T-shirt, his thick hair stylishly disheveled, just as his father's was, in an attempt to look young, whereas the boy looked older than the child he really was in his fashionable attire, brands printed here and there on his body. He scrolled and clicked on his phone until he arrived at the poems.

In truth, I had never really liked him, so precocious and confident. Or maybe I disliked his parents' admiration, the way they always managed to put him in the spotlight without shame.

As the boy was clearing his throat to read, my husband whispered that it was such an honor to listen to a Nobel laureate.

"Shhh," I told him, but I smiled.

The poems were what you might expect from a boy of twelve. There was one from the perspective of a snow leopard, on the brink of extinction. Another about his grandfather and the lessons of his past. The final one was about peace, how it was like a tree that embraced us all in the great sky. The metaphor didn't quite hold up, but I suppose we all understood what he was trying to say.

When he finished reading, Luca bowed, then spun on one heel and walked up to his friends standing next to us. They slapped him on the back. The girl in braces offered him a cookie from her plate.

An older man approached from across the room, saying that the reading was a success. Earlier, I'd seen Anna's husband fetching him food, and I assumed that he was a family member.

"Really good stuff," he declared loudly.

"So great," my husband said. "I loved the grandfather poem."

"These kids are just amazing," the man said. "And that one about peace. You're a good boy, Luca. You're a good boy to think like that."

Luca thanked him. But it seemed that the old man was waiting for something else. He'd moved one step closer, his large abdomen poised between the baby and the teenagers.

"Friends of Anna's?" he asked. He told us he'd known her when she had only two teeth.

"Does this little fellow have any?"

We told him he had none.

"Oh boy, brace yourselves," he said. "Teething is a pain in the ass."

He had two children, grown up. His daughter used to play tennis with Anna when the girls were fifteen.

"Although," he added, "she's gone all woo-woo, now." He waved his hands in the air. "She'll pick a fight over every little thing.

"They used to be great friends," he said. "Anna's a terrific person." It seemed that he held her in higher esteem, for her lack of fighting, perhaps. "They grow up so fast," he said.

"So we've been told," my husband joked. "I have to tell you, it feels pretty slow right now."

"You'll see," the man said. "You'll miss your little baby."

I asked him how often he saw his children.

"All the time," he said. "I was over at my son's last week, to visit the grandkids."

His daughter, he added, was single.

"She's bright," he said. "But she has her opinions."

He really appreciated Luca's poem, he went on. It took a wise little man to wish peace upon everyone. Honestly, he couldn't always find it in himself to do the same.

"Because the way I see it," he said, "there is us. And there is them."

The baby had started fussing, squirming in my arms. My husband took him from me.

"I feel for those people," the man said, "I really do. But we have to defend our way of life."

I said the baby might be getting hungry.

His daughter, he continued, took it upon herself to be a spokesperson for them. She attended demonstrations, organized fundraisers. She went out of her way to make enemies at work. Sometimes he had the sense that she was just a contrarian. Why else would she be so adamant about standing up for a people she had never met?

"Perhaps she wants to ease their suffering," my husband offered.

The old man was silent for a moment.

"Oh, suffering," he said. "There's always some suffering."

I told him I would go and prepare the baby's bottle.

"Good luck with those teeth," he told us, and walked up to another group, in praise of Luca's poetry.

I fed the baby in the bedroom, sitting by the mound of coats. He was hesitant to take the bottle, no doubt startled by the change of scene. I told him it was all right. I was there with him, and we'd go home soon.

"This is a really shitty party," I cooed. "And we got stuck with the racist uncle, didn't we?"

Soon he put his plump hand on mine and pulled the bottle toward himself, gulping while he looked me in the eyes. I was grateful to him. Oh, I was so grateful.

WHEN WE WERE leaving, Anna saw us to the door. She repeated how special it was that we had been able to come.

"I think it was a great success," she said. I thought she was talking about our attendance, before I realized she meant Luca's reading.

"Everyone loved the poems."

There was something indecent about her praise. Not so much that she was boasting about her own child, but that she was able to do so as if talking about a stranger, someone to whom she had no attachment.

Still, we told her that we, too, loved them.

"And I'm just relieved there were no arguments. It's been so tense, you know? It's nice to have a break from all that. Sometimes I just feel like everyone has to relax a little. It's so sad, of course. So sad for everyone. I'm just glad you guys could make it. You're like family to us."

"Thanks, Anna," my husband said, a little brusquely. I kissed her on the cheek. I told her we would talk later.

"You guys teach that baby to sleep," she called after us.

THE BABY FELL asleep on my chest on the bus ride back. My husband and I scrolled on our phones.

"Oh, wow," my husband said, reading the news. "Oh my god." I'd come upon the same story, but I didn't have the heart to read beyond the headlines.

Halfway home, Aziz texted to ask if we'd made it to the party.

Yeah, my husband wrote. *We stopped by for a bit.*

How was it?

Uneventful, my husband wrote back.

What a fucking surprise, Aziz responded. I told my husband not to get into a discussion. Aziz probably wanted to pick an argument, unable to do anything else with the rage he must feel, especially following the day's news. He would certainly have read the whole account that I could not bear to, of the young children abandoned to their fate in bright daylight, fully awake to what was about to befall them.

Aziz, too, had seen his homeland demolished, city by city, though we had never really asked him about the specifics. It seemed improper to pry, and difficult to know what, exactly, to ask.

Later, I told my husband, we would invite him over and tell him that we had found Anna's party a little distasteful; that we were aligned with him in our humanity.

IT WAS AS if we had traveled across the country, rather than made a short bus trip for lunch. It had been nice to get out, we said, without too much conviction.

The baby was not sleepy at bedtime, energized from his nap on the bus. We sat with him on the floor, showing him his toys, stacking and unstacking them. When he finally fell asleep, we fried eggs for dinner and ate them on the couch, where, soon after, I, too, fell asleep.

I woke up to the baby's cries.

It was an earlier request than usual to be brought to bed with us. Most nights, he would sleep for two hours at least before we took him. We worried that if we relented, he'd want to come sooner and sooner, and that we would finally end up having to go to bed with him as we used to.

Still, he continued to cry, so I got up, heading reluctantly for his room.

"Let's just wait a little," my husband said. "Maybe he'll settle."

I sat back down on the edge of the couch as the calls became more desperate.

"He's very tired," my husband said. "He's bound to go back to sleep."

And for a moment, the crying stopped. We looked at each other in disbelief.

"I guess we just needed to give him a minute," I said.

Then it picked back up, with greater force. It was like a siren, almost tranquil in its deafening pitch. I heard in its note of alarm the words of a repeated accusation. As a child, I would decipher the sounds of ambulances and police cars, breaking them down to human speech. Now, as then, I was sure of the meaning of this cry. *You are there*, it exclaimed over and over. *You are there*. I averted my gaze from my husband.

After a while, I got up and went to the bedroom, lest our child know that we were here together, that we were complicit, waiting in silence for his cries to subside.

Twirl

I was sitting in a wine bar waiting for my date when I heard the two women next to me speaking Turkish. My date—it would be our first meeting—had texted to say that he'd be at least thirty minutes late. I considered telling him not to bother, then changed my mind, fearing that I might miss a chance. I pretended to read my book while I listened to the women's conversation. It was such a pleasure to hear my native tongue. I had no Turkish friends in the city; I worked for an arts organization and had befriended my colleagues there, my social circle expanding through their acquaintances in a chain of expats.

The two women were talking about a photography exhibit at one of the city's prominent museums. One of them admired the works' stark shadows and picturesque scenes; the other was dismissive. She told her friend that she found such artistic tricks dishonest. I'd had a similar reaction when I saw the show a few days earlier. I found the photographs too quaint, unnatural.

I was sad to see the women leave, arm in arm. I wished I could join them for dinner, partake in their lively, warm conversation. Whereas the date, when he finally arrived, was entirely unremarkable. I felt I had wasted an evening.

A few days later I saw one of the women—the one who had dismissed the photographs—in my neighborhood. She was leaving the organic store where I also shopped, despite its horrific prices. I could not really afford to shop there, or rather, I could afford only that—my life a facade of beautiful objects and luxurious rituals, without any sturdy foundation.

Hello, I told her. I think you're Turkish?

Even then, when it was no longer a novelty to be away from one's country, there was the instant familiarity, like an obligation.

Ah! she exclaimed. *Merhaba!*

She looked a little older than I had initially guessed. Everything about her was neat and harmonious. *A sign of maturity*, I thought. Someone who had her life together. Her name was Zerrin. Like me, she was from Istanbul.

I confessed to having eavesdropped on her conversation; it had made me happy to hear Turkish.

Zerrin repeated her view that the photos were superficial, despite the great enthusiasm that surrounded them in the media.

Are you interested in art? she asked. I told her about my work. She exclaimed, almost childishly, that we must get together soon.

We have so much to talk about, she said, as if she had decided something about me in these few minutes.

We lived a few blocks apart, on either side of the park, and we agreed to meet in the coming days. Afternoons would be easier, Zerrin explained, somewhat apologetically, because she had a young daughter.

By the evening she'd texted different options, suggesting that we first try one place and, a few days later, another. I was surprised by her enthusiasm, different from the way I had perceived her at the bar.

I'D FINALLY STARTED online dating. The idea had seemed absurd when I was even a year younger, still certain that I would eventually meet someone *naturally*, as if the people encountered through dating sites belonged to a different ecosystem or were not entirely human. But recently I'd begun to feel something close to panic. Still, I dreaded the prospect of meeting strangers from the apps at bars and cafés, trying to gauge in the span of an hour whether they might be worth another date, whether they were safe to go home with, whether the total absence of any common interests might feel less estranging with time. I met with two computer engineers and a historian, each a few years older and unable to ask a single question about me, though I offered them many. By my fourth date, with an Australian musician—that was what he called himself, though I suspected that he mostly played the guitar in his flat—I had started to understand that the more I asked, the more they spoke, mistaking my manners for true interest. To pass the time, I made internal bets about how long I could keep him talking, at what point the indulgence might seem strange even to him. But I could also see that he was turned on by my questions; he loved having a chance to speak, no doubt as I would have as well.

After we finished our drinks, the musician suggested wandering around the neighborhood. I knew already that I wouldn't see him again, but I thought I might kiss him at the end of the evening. As we were reaching my bus stop, he suddenly took my hand and pulled at my arm, twirling me on the pavement. I laughed. It was such a strange gesture, and perhaps also charming; I wasn't sure.

MY FIRST MEETING with Zerrin was at a pub in our neighborhood. From there I would go to another date. I'd decided to line up as many as possible, having heard enough times from my colleagues that this was a numbers game. Some of them had even helped me select photographs for my profile: on a hike, at a café, at the beach wearing a sundress. Friendly, generic pictures that suggested ease, that gave nothing away. I told my colleagues details about physical intimacies, often exaggerated for comical effect.

Sharing any of this with Zerrin seemed inappropriate, even profane. The date would be my first time seeing the man, and I didn't want to risk running into him with Zerrin; I had picked a place a good distance from the pub. What if there was something strange about him, or he was much older than he claimed?

Zerrin approached me, waving from across the street. It was such a pleasure to be reminded of the old familiarities: the warm kiss, the rush to pay for the other's drink, the enthusiasm to establish a connection. As soon as we sat down, we listed favorite spots in Istanbul, quickly finding common acquaintances. Zerrin was wistful. *Not so much for the city*, I thought, *but for the life she'd had there.* Her authority in her native place, her network of friends, her carefree youth. Zerrin's daughter was now starting nursery school—or was it daycare? I didn't really know the difference; I gathered only that the child was still young and that Zerrin was a single parent.

More or less a single parent, she amended. The child's father worked in an adjacent town and came to the city on weekends to spend time with their daughter. Even now, though the child was past the early years of constant care, Zerrin had very little time to herself, and her career had suffered as a result. She was a writer, she told me when I asked. She added hastily that she mainly wrote stories for Turkish literary journals, some of them now defunct, as if she were afraid I might ask her for proof. These days, she said, to make ends meet, she worked on translations in what little time she had.

I told her she was a hero, as is common to say of mothers, especially those who are in a difficult situation.

MY DATE THAT evening was with a high school science teacher. His pictures made him look athletic, in a rugged, nature-loving sort of way. I knew that these profiles rarely matched reality, but I was still disappointed to discover that he was nothing like his photographs. He was unfit and unkempt, with a slouch of self-pity weighing him down. It took him a long time to order: he went back and forth among three options, and when his dish finally arrived, he said he was upset that he'd made the wrong choice. I found them all so childish, these grown men who couldn't see beyond themselves, who were incapable of seduction. This one told me at length about his divorce, the two boys he had on alternate weeks. Then, out of the blue, he reached over to pick something off my shoulder before elaborating on the logistics of his children's visits.

The casual flirtation of the touch was at odds with the man's awkwardness. It puzzled and intrigued me. I thought I must have misread him, that he was not so straightforward as he seemed, and perhaps this was why I agreed to extend our date, walking with him to the metro once we'd paid. But there were no other signs of mystery. Soon after we parted ways, the man texted to ask if I would like to meet up again the following day. I told him I wouldn't.

I thought we had a great time? he wrote.

ZERRIN AND I started to meet on weekday afternoons when I worked from home. We would go to the park, or a café of Zerrin's choosing. I had never experienced the inverted hours of a mother. I found the routine leisurely, if strangely out of time, as if the two of us existed on a different plane while the real world continued a step away—especially because Zerrin knew little about my life outside of our afternoons, and I knew little of hers, I suppose, though I found it easy to imagine.

Tell me everything, she said whenever we met up.

I liked her attention, the yearning with which she asked me about my work, my weekends, my acquaintances. She wanted to know what I did in the evenings, where I went out with my friends. It was so tempting to think of my youth as a virtue.

I used to be just like you, she often told me, relating anecdotes from her student years in Istanbul, when she would be out all night in Cihangir, spend whole days visiting bookshops.

Really—she laughed—I may not look it, but I'm a free spirit at heart!

I found this hard to believe; I continued to be surprised by Zerrin's decorum, her attire, which was always neat, as if she were on her way to an interview. But I told her benevolently that she was still a free spirit.

I WENT ON a date with a man named Kafka. This was the only reason; he didn't look very attractive in his pictures. *Surely*, I thought, *such a name was the sign of an interesting personality.* We met at a rock-climbing gym at the man's suggestion, but we only sat at the bar overlooking the tilted wall. Kafka told me about his father's love for his namesake, as well as his streak of sadism. Who would ever inflict such passions on their child? he asked. He had obviously told this story many times before, but he still acted out the injustice with great fervor. He went on to rank Kafka's works, starting from his favorites, moving down to the ones he considered repetitive or overrated. I didn't agree with him, but I didn't object; he probably had greater authority to evaluate these works—a natural connection. Instead, I pointed out a climber dangling from the slanted wall, holding on with one arm, while his remaining limbs moved about, trying to grasp something. From where we were sitting, the man appeared curiously like an insect, and the prospect of his imminent fall seemed less dramatic.

This was my best date so far. Even though Kafka talked for the majority of the evening, I was interested in what he had to say. He'd become an urban planner, he told me, in utter disregard for where his name might have taken him. Or was it indeed the direct result? He asked which neighborhoods I frequented and told me about little-known parts of these quarters. One favorite, he said, was the courtyard of an old bottle factory, entered through the back door of an Indonesian restaurant. Perhaps he could show me one day.

As he said this, he moved his hand toward my shoulder and picked off a stray hair, which he casually dropped on the floor before smiling at me.

We kissed before parting ways. It was not really an exchange, but not a clash, either. We agreed to meet again.

SOME DAYS LATER, I ran into Zerrin at the organic store. I had already picked out cheeses and olives, good bread and wine. I invited her to my apartment.

Okay, Zerrin said, but let me at least get the wine.

I'd gone shopping with Kafka in mind, in case he came over following our outing to the old bottle factory, but it seemed more fun to share my small feast with Zerrin. And of course there was vanity: I wanted her to see my flat, its careful decoration and charm, my life as an independent, single woman.

Zerrin was enchanted. That's what she kept saying, that my place was enchanting. I should consider myself lucky to have found it: the city was becoming unaffordable. She could never live in this neighborhood if she were to move in today. I wondered whether, like me, Zerrin was living beyond her means for the sake of being central, not feeling left out.

She examined my books, my assortment of mugs, the trinkets on the shelves, asking me where I'd gotten them, what they signified to me. There was no self-consciousness in her avid regard, no attempt to hide her curiosity.

Everything is so beautiful, she said. And again when I'd arranged the cheeses on a board with fruits and handed her a glass of wine.

When she was a student, she told me, she always had friends over. They would eat and drink, sometimes smoke a cigarette or two, she said giddily, as if announcing a great secret. She lived in a beautiful flat in Arnavutköy. It was the favored meeting spot among her classmates.

They'd just show up, she said, knock knock, no warning! Sometimes they stayed the night. We used to joke that I was running a hostel.

Sounds so fun, I told her.

Really, Zerrin said, you would've loved it. We should've met two decades ago!

•

THE NEXT DAY Kafka showed me the courtyard, pointing out the details of its industrial past, and from there we walked through a farmer's market that extended several blocks. There were food carts and musicians; a cheerful scene that put us both in a good mood. We got wine from a stall, pastries from another. Just as we had finished our drinks and were approaching a jazz trio in old-timey clothes, Kafka reached for my hand and pulled at it, eventually managing to twirl me. I was taken aback, remembering the twirl from several weeks earlier—the surprise of it, my clumsy step to follow the man's lead. Still, I reasoned, this was a little different. There was music playing, people swaying from side to side. A little girl was also twirling, alone, in front of the collection hat.

We kissed again. I invited him over, warning him that I could offer only the remains of a bottle of wine.

Bottle remains are my favorite offering, Kafka said.

There wasn't a long prelude to sex. Afterward he left to meet his friends for dinner.

In the following weeks, we got together several more times: at my place, or at a restaurant before coming home. We enjoyed similar foods; we always found a topic to discuss. I thought, with optimism, that there was something there. Or there would be, given enough time.

•

I HADN'T SEEN Zerrin since her visit. She messaged frequently to ask how I was doing and sent articles she thought I might enjoy.

Tell me when you'd like to meet up, she finally wrote. *I know you must be very busy.*

I found her message strangely needy. Still, the next time we got together, I explained to her that I'd met someone—through mutual friends, I lied—and had been spending a lot of time with him.

Zerrin clapped her hands at my news. We were having tea at my flat. Once again, I had taken care to make a nice presentation. I filled an old porcelain dish with cherries, put out little bowls of nuts and biscuits.

I recounted the early date to the bottle factory and our long walk afterward.

Isn't it so fun to be in love? Zerrin said childishly.

During their first years as a couple, she told me, she and her husband used to discover faraway corners of Istanbul, walking for entire days, making stops here and there to read or have coffee. Later, they had traveled all over the world, to India, Cambodia, Brazil. They always explored by foot, considering it the best way to get acquainted with a new place. But they were different people back then, and though she retained the spirit of her former self, she could barely recognize that energetic, curious man in her husband.

You mean your ex-husband? I asked.

Well, Zerrin said, we aren't officially separated. It's just a formality, she added. Their relationship was entirely drained of affection, but their daughter was still too young to sever bonds completely.

I asked if it was difficult for her to see him on the weekends, when he came to the city.

We can still spend time together, she said. He stays with us, after all.

I hadn't realized that, I said. It was very generous of her to allow it.

There's no big drama, she told me. In fact, they were perfectly civil. It was a state of mind. At some point, it had dawned on her that the marriage had ended and they were only performing a series of gestures they'd committed to memory.

I was interested in this; the internal knowledge. I told her that I often had trouble judging whether a relationship had substance. I could be naive, I said, or oblivious.

Not at all, Zerrin said. You know how to enjoy life. You know how to retain your freedom. You're doing all the right things.

I was flattered, so I didn't object. I asked how she'd known that her marriage was over.

I suppose a child changes everything, Zerrin said. After the birth, their union had become unbalanced, the sacrifices one-sided. They hadn't been able to recover their carefree friendship. Perhaps she was even to blame. She'd been too complacent.

I didn't know how to respond. I felt so removed from her experience, and perhaps I found it a little pathetic that she had not been able to stand her ground. But I repeated what I'd told her a few weeks earlier, that she was a hero.

Zerrin shrugged.

Enjoy every minute with your boyfriend, she said.

As she was leaving my apartment that afternoon, she remarked that there were a lot of bees outside, pointing to the small swarm hovering around the potted plants in the courtyard.

Strange to see so many of them in the city, she said. It's kind of refreshing.

I didn't understand what she meant by this, and I didn't ask. I needed to start preparing for the evening, when I would meet Kafka at a Korean place in his neighborhood. This was always my favorite part of a date—the anticipation, the dressing up. As I was putting on earrings, I noticed that the bees had increased in number, moving blotches against my bedroom window. An hour later, the window frame was covered in a thick swarm, slowly swallowing the glass.

I called Kafka to tell him I would be late. There were now several hundred bees in the courtyard, and I could not imagine stepping out without being stung. But surely, I added, they would drift off in a bit.

Let's just postpone, he proposed. He said that the situation with the bees sounded really bizarre.

What should I do about it? I asked. I'm trapped here.

I guess you'll have to wait it out, he said.

I then took a photo and sent it to Zerrin.

Bees took me hostage, I wrote. Immediately, she suggested coming over to bring me food. I told her it was out of the question. Still, I wished Kafka might at least have offered to do the same.

Soon after, Zerrin wrote that she'd contacted an apiculturist in the area and that someone would be arriving shortly.

As I waited, I pressed my face against the window, feeling a vertiginous thrill. The bees tumbled past my cheeks and mouth, their whirs audible through the glass. At first, it seemed that they were walking drunkenly on top of each other. After a while, however, I saw their small wiggles and turns; the careful dance each of them performed in the little space they had. I watched, mesmerized, my face numb against their bodies.

An hour later, a middle-aged woman carrying a large bag appeared in the courtyard. She donned her white suit, then opened two jars of honey. Within minutes she had gathered the bees to herself, the insects at once frantic and serene, buzzing around her lifted arms. I came out of the apartment to thank her.

Always a nice way to end an evening, she said. With my little friends.

I told her that her little friends had imprisoned me in my own home.

You should take it as a good sign, she said. These remarkable creatures are very picky about their environments. She was a lawyer, but her real passion had always been bees.

Remarkable little creatures, she repeated.

I texted Kafka that I was liberated, but he had made other plans. He was busy that weekend, too, so I arranged to spend Saturday with colleagues. I suggested going to the farmer's market, after which I could show them the old bottle factory. Once again, the market was lively, with music and cheerful stalls. I directed our group toward the drinks stand.

The aphrodisiac, one of them joked. I'd told them about my second date with Kafka, how we'd ended up at my place that afternoon.

Watch out, I said. Might hit you any minute. Just then, I saw Kafka across the street, holding hands with a woman in a floral dress. As I made to hurriedly look away, he lifted the woman's arm and twirled her in one swoop.

Really, it was a gorgeous sight. Kafka stood still, his hand raised in a perfect arc. He caught his partner's gaze just as she was twirling. For a second, their eyes locked. The woman's skirt billowed, wrapped around her thighs, then dropped. This must have been how it was supposed to look; it was so much the right move.

In the evening, I looked it up online: *twirling, first date, pickup moves*. Within seconds, I was reading a list of ways to ensure a successful date. On a first meeting, the website instructed, you should casually remove something off your date's clothing. Even if there was nothing, you could always pretend to spot a strand of hair, a leaf, a piece of lint. This would create a sense of organic intimacy, from which you could build: touching the woman's arm to emphasize a point, patting her on the back, taking her hand on a walk. All these steps would come naturally if the foundation of physical intimacy was established early on. A few items down, I read that twirling one's date out of the blue could signal spontaneity and fun, and make a woman feel like a heroine, playing the lead role.

The following day, even though I hadn't heard from him, I texted Kafka that I didn't want to see him again.

Ah! he wrote back. *I've had a lovely time with you.*

ZERRIN AND I were at the beginning of a walk one Friday when her daughter's school called to say that there had been an accident. Her daughter had fallen and lost a tooth. She had cried considerably and was still unsettled. Zerrin said she would be over immediately, and I offered to come along. Ever since the incident with the bees, I'd wanted to do something nice for her.

There were more tears at the reunion; the daughter released the final shock of her fall. Then her attention turned to me. She was pleased there was a new person on their outing. She announced that she was hungry.

How about a yummy slice of cake? I proposed. There was a very good bakery some blocks down at the edge of the park; I would treat us all.

I know the one, Zerrin said.

The child took my hand. Her palm was warm and sticky, and I felt strangely honored. We ate our cakes sitting on a bench, in front of the grand houses lining one side of the street.

How's the great romance? Zerrin asked.

Hardly that, I said. For some reason, I couldn't bring myself to tell her, just yet, that it had ended so quickly. I was even more reluctant now that I knew the seduction had been an illusion, repeated time after time. And that I'd been deceived, so easily.

Oh, you're in *love*! Zerrin said. I can see it in your *eyes*.

No, I told her. I'm really not. I'm not even sure we're a good match.

But he sounds so fun.

I suppose so.

The child had taken my hand again and was tugging at it.

Let's go to my room, she said, as if we were already at home.

Darling, Zerrin said, she probably has other things to do.

No! the child shouted, pulling me more forcefully. Come and see my room!

I told Zerrin I didn't mind. The attention of a child had always made me feel accomplished. Besides, I had a date with someone new in a few hours and would be glad to kill time.

You don't have to humor her, Zerrin said, but I was already following the daughter's lead. Zerrin sat a while longer on the bench before finally getting up.

It turned out that we were in fact sitting right across from their house, a two-story villa with vast windows I'd often admired from that very spot at the edge of the park. I could barely contain my surprise. I'd assumed a different life for Zerrin—a single parent who didn't work. Perhaps her insistence that my apartment was full of charm had made me think that hers must be lacking it.

As she was taking out keys in her bag, Zerrin mumbled that her husband might be home for the weekend.

He was. Stocky and cheerful, he greeted us in a blue canvas apron.

Where's my ninja turtle? he asked. The child ran to show him the site of her broken tooth.

Oh no! he said. We'll have to glue it back!

He slung her on his shoulder, to the child's shrieking delight, then kissed Zerrin on the cheek. She didn't protest.

I tried to look at her for some explanation, but Zerrin was busy taking off her coat, putting away the child's bag.

After I'd seen the room—unsparingly pink—I sat at the kitchen island with a glass of wine. Zerrin had disappeared upstairs, seemingly in a hurry to tend to something. The house was lavishly spacious. There were long corridors of closed doors, accented with paintings, and plants the size of small trees. There must have been servants, too, to keep everything spotless, continuously erasing the usual signs of life and wear.

Zerrin's husband was frying halloumi. There was a shopping bag on the counter; bowls and utensils; packs of washed, perfectly shaped vegetables.

I offered to help.

I got this, he said. Friday's my day to cook. Helps me relax.

Are you ready for the weekend? he said. I sure am.

I told him I was hoping to see friends. Perhaps a movie.

He nodded as if he'd already known my answer.

I asked if he had plans.

Nothing at all. Not. One. Thing. Put up my feet. Be with the girls.

It was so nice to be back home, he continued. I might already know from Zerrin that he spent weekdays in another town. He had a small flat close to his work, which he used like a hotel. The long weekly commute and the days away from his family felt particularly difficult this year. It would be so much easier if Zerrin agreed to move to the countryside. But she'd always been a city girl.

Anyway, he said, I'm going to start looking for a place in the country soon. Whatever Zerrin says. When you're making good money, he chuckled, you have to be able to enjoy it.

Zerrin came to the kitchen briefly, then left. From the hallway, she called out to her husband that he should offer me a drink.

I already have one, I called back. I'm very well taken care of.

Soon after this, I announced that I would get going. At the door, Zerrin kissed me goodbye.

You have a beautiful home, I told her.

Zerrin waved her hand abstractly.

Come again for dinner, the husband shouted. I never get to meet Zerrin's friends.

I STILL HAD some time until my date and decided to take a roundabout path through the park. The sun was setting; deep shadows stretched gently into every furrow. The call of the mourning doves rang from treetops. I was glad to be alone.

I knew already that I wouldn't ask Zerrin about any of it—the grand house, or the husband's oblivion to the separation she'd described. It would be an embarrassment for both of us. Besides, I reasoned, the situation wasn't so different from what she had told me. Not quite a lie but a deliberate presentation of facts.

At the other end of the park I put on lipstick, checking the contours on my phone screen. Then I continued to the intersection where we'd agreed to meet. The man was already there, standing with his hands in his pockets. He didn't take them out when he saw me. We walked for a while, looking for a place to sit down, finally settling on a craft beer bar. The conversation was neither engaging nor terrible; I knew what questions to ask to enliven our time together.

Afterward we walked a bit more. The park was locked for the night, so we traced the periphery, passing by Zerrin's house, which was dark save for a dim light coming from the second floor. I slowed my step to look up, though it was unlikely I would get a glimpse of the family. The child would be asleep, the husband and wife tending to their own lives. Surely it wasn't such an unappealing fate.

I had the sense that I'd been thrown off a ship. I wondered at Zerrin's ready admiration of my life; it seemed now that she'd been humoring me. Without her eager audience, my youth felt charmless. It was already spent.

We passed the organic shop and were turning toward my street. In a moment, I would make up my mind to invite the man over. Just then, I felt the familiar tug and raised my arm to follow its lead.

ACKNOWLEDGMENTS

My heartfelt thanks to Sarah Bowlin, Callie Garnett, Cressida Leyshon, Deborah Treisman, Sophie Missing, for hearing the voices of these stories and helping to make them come alive. It has been a privilege working with you.

Thank you also to Suzanne Keller, Amanda Dissinger, Harriett Collins, and the teams at Bloomsbury and Scribner.

Adam Dalva, Meghan O'Rourke, Brendan Barrington, Emily Nemens, Hasan Altaf, Imogen Greenhalgh, Meakin Armstrong: I am grateful for your support.

To my friends who have read these stories over the years, whose conversations offer new ways of looking at the world.

Fuat, İsmihan, and Adıhan, my earliest companions in storytelling and observation.

Maks, my first, most trusted reader.

A NOTE ON THE AUTHOR

AYŞEGÜL SAVAŞ is the author of the acclaimed novels *The Anthropologists*, *White on White*, and *Walking on the Ceiling*, and the nonfiction book *The Wilderness*. Her work has been translated into ten languages and has appeared in the *New Yorker*, the *Paris Review*, *Granta*, and elsewhere. She lives in Paris.